ELECTION MISDIRECTION

MIDDLE SCHOOL MAYHEM: BOOK NINE

C.T. WALSH

FARCICAL PRESS

COVER CREDITS

Cover design by Books Covered
Cover photographs © Shutterstock
Cover illustrations by Maeve Norton

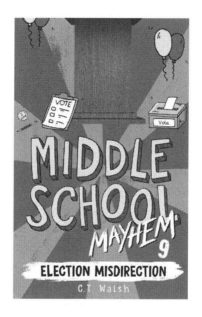

For my Family

Thank you for all of your support

Some people think that high school is even worse than middle school. I think that's for each person to decide for themselves. What I can tell you is that doing middle school AND high school at the same time is worse than either of them on their own. Yep. I did that. You wanna know how to ruin a kid's summer vacation? The summer vacation where said kid is heading into eighth grade, looking forward to ruling the school after two years of a mayhem-enduring monstrosity? You tell that poor child, who still has that wonder in his eyes, that his former-favorite science teacher, Mr. Gifford, who is now dead to him, recommended that the poor youth start first period in high-school science instead of in middle school with his amazing girlfriend as his lab partner.

Oh, and when you go and sprinkle a political election on top of the whole thing, I assure you, it's mayhem. It went something like this. I present only the facts. No embellishments, distortions, or outright lies. Just like all my other stories.

I had to be out of the house an hour earlier than the year

before. High school already stunk, and I hadn't even started yet. The bus ride was better than middle school, probably because it was so early that most teens were still zombies at that point. Plus, my sister, Leighton was in eleventh grade and popular, so while she was embarrassed of me, most of the kids knew not to mess with me.

I had science first period and then I was to head over to the middle school, which was within walking distance. I had many fears. The three most important ones were running into my former middle school principal, current high school principal, and arch nemesis, Principal Buthaire, (You can call him Butt Hair if you want. I do.), navigating a school with kids up to five years older than me and a foot taller, and leaving Sophie behind in science, my love and lab partner.

I didn't know who my new lab partner would be, but I

was pretty certain love would not be in the cards. And that was before I met him.

I sat by myself on the bus, which was fine, but my sister caught up to me as we exited the bus onto the sidewalk.

"Keep your head down and try to fit in," she said, like there was no way I would ever fit in. "And if you see me in the halls, pretend you don't see me."

"Thanks for the pep talk," I said.

"Freshmen are the lowest of the low and you're lower than that. You're a dork who's skipping a grade."

"Just one class. And thanks again for all your support."

Leighton said, "That's not how I see you. That's how everybody else will see you, though. High school is pretty judgy."

I nodded.

Leighton looked at me sympathetically and said, "Count to five and then head into school."

"Why?" I asked, nervously. "Am I gonna self-destruct?" Maybe I had watched too many spy movies.

"That's up to you," she said, walking away. "Start counting now."

"Sister afraid to be seen with you, too?" a familiar voice said.

I turned to see Barney Herbert, who was standing beside me. Barney was a core member of Nerd Nation. He was the former treasurer of the robotics club. He was a nice kid. And if you believe my sister, was the lowest of the low, heading into school for his first day as a freshman.

"What's up, Barn Door?" I asked. It was a nickname he had been given and actually liked since elementary school, on account that his name was Barney and he was always walking into walls and doors. He was just a tad clumsy.

"I've got the first-day jitters," he said, as we headed into the school lobby. "More so than the regular, every-day nerd jitters."

"You'll be fine," I said. "I'm nervous, too."

Despite the less-than-inspiring motivation from Leighton, I felt a strange combination of optimism and nervousness. I would miss Sophie, but we still had lunch, math, and health together in the second half of the year. I was concerned about Butt Hair getting in my own hair, but how bad could it be, only being in the school for one period a day?

As we entered the lobby, I looked around. I had been in the high school before, but never while it was packed with kids. It was like middle school, but on steroids. I was looking into everyone's backs. I had grown a few inches over the past year, but it was like the whole school was one enormous basketball team.

"I can handle this," Barney said. "This is my time," he said, seemingly trying to psyche himself up.

The crowd was packed pretty tight, as all of the buses had let out at the same time and we all funneled into the same handful of doors. I furrowed my brow as I heard the squeaking of shoes and a few yelps up ahead.

"What's going on?" I asked, standing up on my tippy toes. "I can't see anything."

"Don't know, but it's coming this way," Barney said.

He was right. Whatever the commotion was, it was coming our way. And fast. The only problem? There was nowhere to go. We were basically shoulder to shoulder. And then the crowd in front of us parted like the Red Sea. Kids were diving to the sides to avoid what was coming our way. I let out a primal scream and jumped to my left, but it was to no avail.

Two giant dudes held poles with a six-foot wall of duct

tape that stretched from pole to pole. They ran at us at lightning speed. My eyes widened as I soared through the air with my three-inch vertical jump. Despite my considerable athletic prowess, the duct tape attack was too strong. The tape wall slammed into Barney and me. I struggled as the giant dudes carried us across the lobby, seemingly without strain, as they ran full speed while Barney and I dangled from the tape trap.

My whole, short life flashed before my eyes. Most of the images were Derek sitting on my head and farting, which was disappointing. Certainly, I could've thought of better stuff to think about before heading to the afterlife.

2

High school hadn't even officially started, and I was already in the Dork-of-the-Month Club. Barney and I dangled from the wall, duct tape pinning us to it. A web of duct tape ran from my knees all the way up to my neck. I struggled, but couldn't break free as a crowd started to form around us.

"This is a good start to high school," Barney said.

I wasn't sure if he was just trying to talk himself into it again or if he really believed it. "You serious?"

"At least they know who we are."

"I'd rather be invisible. Like right now."

"Hey, how's it going? I'm Barney. You can call me, Barn Door, if you want."

"What are you doing?" I whispered.

"We're socializing here. I think this is gonna be good for us. You gotta look on the bright side of things."

I looked out into the crowd and saw my sister. She was staring back at me, mortified. I would've waved, but still couldn't move my arms. She had complete control of all her appendages and, much to my chagrin, implemented the face palm.

Kids were laughing with each other, pointing and analyzing our situation, like we were some sort of art exhibit.

"It's so lifelike," Airhead Amanda said. She was Ditzy Dayna's sister and shared her brain power, or lack thereof. "Is this from the summer art program?"

The laughing and pointing continued until the familiar, squeaky voice of Principal Buthaire said, "What's so funny, Camels?" He wasn't trying to insult them. Our high school team name was the Courageous Camels. As if enduring being a Gopher in middle school wasn't bad enough. On the plus side, I got to be both at the same time. Lucky me.

Kid scattered like bugs under a giant, stomping boot. Principal Butt Hair pushed his way through the crowd. A smile spread across his face as he saw mine.

"Misterrrr Davenport, I've missed you so. Handing out detentions to students other than you just doesn't do it for me."

Any hopes of staying under the radar or even starting fresh with the Prince of Butt Hair were totally shot. It was just the three of us at that point. All of the other kids had disappeared. As fun as it probably was to see two doofuses dangle from the wall, there was a lot more downside if you got on the wrong side of Principal Buthaire. I was living proof of that. And I hadn't even done anything wrong, which was the most annoying part of it all. Someone had warned him about my brother, Derek, and somehow, he mistook me for him, despite the fact that I don't have the family butt chin. It's a long story.

"Can we get down now?" I asked.

"Feel free," Principal Buthaire said, chuckling to himself.

I realized the joke, even though I didn't find it funny. We needed help to get down.

Principal Buthaire looked at Barney and asked, "And who might you be?"

"Barney Herbert, sir," the Barn Door said, nervously.

"You've chosen interesting company."

"Can you get someone to let us down?" I asked, annoyed.

"Not before you tell me who did this," Prince Butt Hair said, somewhat frustrated.

I studied him. He had aged much more than the few months or so since I had last seen him. Wrinkles had started to spread across his forehead, and he had gray hair at his temples and in his bushy mustache.

"It's good to see that your mustache has grown back so

nicely," I said. It was the one thing I could appreciate about him. He had a solid 'stache, something every middle school boy wanted more than anything.

Butt Hair rolled his eyes. It probably wasn't a great reminder for him. Amanda Gluskin ripped the left side of his mustache off with duct tape, which, among other things, nearly got me expelled from Cherry Avenue Middle School and ended up getting Butt Hair reassigned.

"Who did this and where did they go?" Principal Buthaire said, his tone growing angry.

"I don't know the answers," I said.

"And you, Misterrrr Herbert?"

Bad news for Barney. Principal Buthaire fully associated him with me. He was extending the 'r' in mister, which up until that point, was something he only did when he was angry with me, which was pretty much every time he looked at me.

"I've never seen any of them before. And they disappeared through the front doors."

"Lying about crime details is obstruction of justice and a punishable offense, Misterrrr Davenport." It was great to see he hadn't changed a bit since we last met.

"I wasn't lying. I just didn't see where they went."

"It's an unlikely story. I'll have Cheeks the Custodian cut you down when he has some time."

"How long will that be?" I asked.

"Long enough that you'll be late," Principal Butt Hair said, smiling. He pulled out his detention pad, filled out two of them, and used the edge of the duct tape to stick them to the wall. "Have a great first day!"

"Thanks!" Barn Door said.

I wasn't as enthused. I watched helplessly as Principal Buthaire strutted away, obviously pleased with himself.

3

It took Cheeks a solid ten minutes to cut us down and extract the considerable amount of tape from our bodies. He was not as friendly as Zorch, my middle school custodian who had bailed me out of a bunch of jams much like this one.

Eventually, I found my way to the science wing and tentatively walked into class. Twenty-four students and Miss Kelvin all stared at me, as I entered and slipped into an empty desk in the back of the class.

"Welcome!" Miss Kelvin said, giving me attention that I most certainly didn't want. She seemed nice, anyway. A bit disheveled, with her curly hair scattered all about and her coke-bottle glasses crooked on her nose.

"Thank you," I said, as softly as possible.

"That's the kid who got duct-taped," some dude whispered to laugher across the room.

Duct Tape Davenport. That was me. Hey, it was better than what my arch nemesis, Randy Warblemacher, called me. In case you don't know or don't remember, he called me, Davenfart.

"Before we break up into lab partners, did everyone have a good summer? I read a book on anti-gravity. I couldn't put it down..."

I chuckled and then looked around at the room, staring at me. Nobody else seemed to get the joke. It didn't stop Miss Kelvin from telling another one.

"What does a subatomic duck say?" Miss Kelvin looked around the room. "Anybody?"

Against my better judgement, I raised my hand. "A Quark?"

Miss Kelvin broke out into a snort. I thought a pig had run into the room or something. It wouldn't be out of the question in my experience. "That is correct."

The rest of the class stared at me again. It was starting to get annoying.

"Where does bad light end up? Anybody?" She looked at me. I didn't want to answer. She shrugged and said, laughing, "In prism. Get it?"

"Miss Kelvin?" the annoying kid asked.

"Yes, Martin?"

"Where did you go to college?"

"Duke University."

Martin cupped his ear. "Did you say, Dork?"

A few kids laughed.

"Duke," Miss Kelvin corrected.

"Dork?"

"Duke."

"Dork?"

"Duke."

"Oh, you're talking about Dork U?"

Well, it looked like I found the Randy of the ninth-grade class.

The girl next to me asked, "Are you one of those kid

geniuses who comes up from fourth grade and like next year you'll be in college or something?"

I shrugged. "I'm in eighth grade, just a year ahead in science."

"Oh, that's not impressive at all. I thought you were in elementary school."

I shrugged again and hoped that she would not be my lab partner.

Miss Kelvin stumbled through the rows of desks, knocking into each one, pairing off lab partners. By the time she got to me, I wondered how she was still standing with her hips taking so much punishment, but she was a power-house, and kept going.

"Why don't you three work together?" Miss Kelvin said, pointing to me and the hulking dude next to me.

"There's only two of us," I said.

She took a step back and nearly fell over the annoying girl next to me, which wouldn't be the worst thing in the world. Miss Kelvin looked at the dude next to me and said, "You're one kid?"

It was a weird question for sure, but the kid, who was more man than kid, said, 'Miss Kelvin, it's me, Flea?"

"Oh, Flea! So good to see you. You've grown. Why don't you work with this tiny little fellow here?" She looked at me. "What's your name?"

"Austin Davenport," I said, quietly.

"Oh, our genius! Everybody, this is Austin! He's up from eighth grade to take science with us. He comes highly recommended by the debonair Mr. Gifford." Miss Kelvin's face turned a pinkish hue.

"Big deal," the duct-tape tattler, Martin, said.

Flea stuck out his hand for a shake. I took it as Miss

Kelvin walked or stumbled to the front of the room. I shook Flea's hand. It was twice the size of mine. My fingers crunched from the strength of his grip.

I held in the pain and forced a smile. "Nice to meet you, Flea. It's just Flea?"

"Yep. I'm the smallest in my family."

"How did Miss Kelvin know you?"

"This is my fourth year in ninth-grade science."

It was gonna be a great year in high school science.

After class was over, I hustled out of the high school and over to middle school. I went as fast as I could. When I got there, I pulled open the door, entering like I had just broken an Olympic track record.

"And the crowd goes wild..." I looked around. "Where is everyone? Ugh. I'm late." I was hoping to see my friends in the Atrium before Advisory started. It was my favorite time at school. I had more time with them during lunch, but at least before school I didn't have the potential downside of death like I did in the cafeteria. It did keep things interesting, though.

4

I ninjaed (is that a word?) my way through the hallway. I was late and didn't want to be the first kid to get detention in both middle and high school on the same day. Thankfully, I made it through the Atrium and down the hallway to my Advisory class. I slipped into the room and into the seat behind my buddy, Just Charles. Yes, we called him that. He's not a Charlie and he's certainly not a Chuck.

There wasn't a whole lot going on. I apparently hadn't missed much.

Just Charles turned around to face me. "Missed you this morning. What is that all over your clothes?"

"Umm, glue?"

"I thought you were taking science in high school not art?"

"It's a long story." At least it was better than when I got glitter-bombed by Amanda Gluskin during the science fair.

And then the Speaker of Doom crackled, readying to give us the bad news of the day: what rules have changed to make our lives more miserable; what cafeteria food might potentially kill us that day; and for me, it often led to being called down to the principal's office for an undeserved tongue lashing and detention.

Dr. Dinkledorf's voice boomed through the speaker, "Welcome to our incoming sixth graders and welcome back to our returning students! We hope you have a fabulous year. I have one important announcement for our eighth graders. Should you wish to run for President in the school election, it will be held in two weeks. You can get a signature sheet from the main office or me, Dr. Dinkledorf. You need twenty-five signatures by Friday to participate. You will have to give two speeches and participate in a debate, in addition to whatever other campaigning you choose to do."

Just Charles turned to me again. "You gonna run?"

"Absolutely not. I want no part of that. You?"

"Nah, man. Same."

"What about Evil Chuck?" I asked. It was Just Charles' alter ego that surfaced once he hit a certain intake of sugar. We were still trying to figure out where his limit was, but it seemed to change each time.

"He'd be a terrible president. He would most certainly abuse his power."

"He'd still be better than Randy."

"True, but so would most dictators throughout history," Just Charles said.

I didn't disagree.

∼

I FINALLY GOT to see Sophie at lunch in fourth period. I already didn't like my schedule and was regretting high school science, not that it was my choice.

I met Ben, Sophie, Cheryl, and Luke at our usual table. I threw my tray onto the table.

"What is curious chicken? Why can't we start the year with a solid pizza bagel?"

"You can't go wrong with a pizza bagel," Ben said. "You have to try to mess that up. But I wouldn't put it past them."

"How was high school, hot shot?" Sophie asked.

"Ahh, well, I've had better days," I said.

"It was one period. What could've happened?"

"I got detention. And I was kinda sorta duct taped to the wall with Barney Herbert."

"Oh, no!" Sophie said.

"And then what happened?" Cheryl asked while Luke laughed.

"We were stuck. Butt Hair gave me detention for being late to class, which is par for the course, and then I went to class. It was pretty uneventful."

"You think it was the same crew that took down Principal Puma?"

"Who knows?" I said, shrugging. "Principal Butt Hair looked like he's aged a lot. Whoever it is, he hasn't been able to stop them."

"I'm sure it'll get better," Sophie said. "In other news, I've decided that I'm running for class president. What do you think?" she asked, excitedly.

"I'm behind you a hundred percent. I will be your campaign manager," I said.

"That sounds awesome," Luke said. "You'll do great."

Sophie looked at me and said, "I want you to be my chief strategist. Cheryl will be campaign manager."

Ben asked, "Why do you even want to run? It's just a popularity contest."

"Because I want to create change. Have you seen the food they make us eat? I think the nutritional value of half this stuff is negative. And the other half might not even be food."

"Yeah, this chicken is mighty curious," I said, pushing it around with my fork. "I think people could get behind a campaign like that."

"Where's Sammie, by the way?" Cheryl asked Ben.

"She should be here any minute. She had to do something for cheerleading."

And he was right. Sammie strolled in with her tray and sat down next to Ben.

"Curious chicken? That's the best thing on the menu?"

"It's very curious," I said.

Sammie didn't look happy.

Ben asked, "You okay?"

"Well, we'll see what happens after I eat this, but when I dropped off some paperwork to Miss Dexter, I heard some of the cheerleaders talking about Regan, saying she's starting some secret club, The Pretty Posse. Invitation only."

"Did you get an invite?" Ben asked.

"No. They don't include me in stuff because I'm friends with..."

"Me?" I asked.

"Pretty much."

"Sorry," I said.

"I don't want to be included in their stupid stuff, especially something like that. I mean, some of the girls are nice. Others like Regan, I want nothing to do with."

"The Pretty Posse," Sophie said. "That's just wrong."

"Can you introduce me to some of them?" Luke asked.

"Typical," Sammie said, shaking her head.

～

We survived the curious chicken, at least for the next few periods, anyway. I had the pleasure of my first run in with Randolph Newton Warblemacher. I saw his smug face approaching down the hall.

"Davenfart! I almost missed you this summer, but now that I can smell you, I'm not sure why."

"Randolph, always a displeasure to see you," I said, continuing my walk toward class.

"I'm running for president and I'm gonna crush you."

I laughed and kept going.

"What's so funny?" Randy said, more annoyed than curious, as he turned and followed me down the hall.

I wasn't going to tell him that I wasn't running. I saluted him. "I know you'll serve yourself well!" His time in power as a Peer Review Counselor under Principal Buthaire's unfair Student Behavior System that he had implemented the year prior was proof of that.

"You're not gonna run against me?" Randy asked, disappointed.

"You have bigger problems than me running, Rancid Randy."

"Rancid?"

"Yeah, you stink."

Randy sniffed his shirt. "No, I don't!"

I laughed as I walked into my math class to meet Sophie.

5

I had the pleasure of ending the day in gym class, a nerd's favorite subject. Sophie and I walked toward the gym together. It was the first time we saw the Pretty Posse in full swing. Regan Storm, Randy's on-again, off-again girlfriend, and wicked witch of Cherry Avenue, strutted in front of four girls. Regan's hair blew behind her like she was on a photo shoot, like it always did. She was flanked on both sides by carbon copies, leaving middle school boys in a heap of love.

Regan smirked when she saw us. "Oh, look, it's the most annoying couple in the school." The Pretty Posse laughed. She could say, "Look, there's the library," and they probably would've thought it was hilarious.

"I think that title goes to you and Randy," I said.

"Whatever, nerd," Regan said, blowing past us.

Sophie turned and was about to say something, but I grabbed her arm and pulled. They didn't have the best of histories, and Regan Storm was certainly not worth getting angry over.

I headed into the gym and my day (and year) got better (insert eye roll). Randy was sitting in the stands with a group of football players. I was gonna have to endure his idiocy all year in gym class.

Thankfully, Ben and Just Charles were in my class as well. We would endure the pain together, forming a nerd support group for whomever needed help.

As we waited for our esteemed gym teacher, Mr. Muscalini, to grace us with his biceps and quads, Randy decided to continue his push for my presidency.

"Hey, Davenfart! I was thinking about our conversation from before," he called out for all of the forty or so kids in the gym to hear. "I was thinking you're probably just scared to run against me, which is understandable. But you're the king of the nerds. That ought to count for something."

The clowns around him started to laugh. Plus a few other kids who were scattered around the gym.

"Nah, I'm good, man. Thanks for the kind words, though."

I looked away from Randy and over to Ben and Just Charles.

"How angry is he?" I whispered.

"On Randy's scale of one to ten, I'd say about a six," Ben said.

"Agreed," Just Charles added.

Before any more nonsense occurred, the locker room door swung open, seemingly almost ripped right out of the door jamb. Mr. Muscalini, our overmuscled physical education teacher, strode into the center of the gym. He wore his typical too-short shorts, revealing his tree trunk-sized quads.

"I've been looking forward to this all summer!" Mr. Muscalini's voice boomed as he faced us. "I want to start the school year off right and with a bang. It's gonna be a dodge-ball extravaganza! Dodge ball, all month long!"

Kyle "Cry Baby" Crawford literally fell to the ground and, of course, started sobbing. I didn't feel so hot, either.

"What? Really?" Just Charles asked.

"It builds character," I said, sarcastically.

"It breaks bones and spirits," Ben countered.

The dodgeball extravaganza did not live up to Mr.

Muscalini's hype, at least for those of us who don't normally play sports and enjoy trying to blow other people's heads to smithereens with rubber balls. We formed our usual nerd herd, but I still got pummeled. It kind of summed up my day.

I met up with Sophie in the Atrium before it was time to hop on the afternoon bus. "Randy is on my case to run in the election."

"You're not going to do it, right?" Sophie asked, concerned.

"No. I have no interest. And you're the best candidate for the job, so I want you to win."

Sophie exhaled. "Do you think Ben is right, that it's just a popularity contest?"

"It is, probably to a lot of kids, but not to everyone."

"I hope they like me."

"How could they not?"

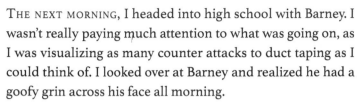

THE NEXT MORNING, I headed into high school with Barney. I wasn't really paying much attention to what was going on, as I was visualizing as many counter attacks to duct taping as I could think of. I looked over at Barney and realized he had a goofy grin across his face all morning.

"Why are you so happy?" I asked.

"I got duct taped to Melissa Mittlestadt in the cafeteria yesterday. We bonded. I think I'm gonna ask her out."

I wasn't sure who she was, but if he was happy, I was happy for him. And he didn't ask me for any love advice, which was a positive, because I was still fresh out after Valentine's Day. Don't ask.

As we headed into the lobby and waded through the crowds, shrieks echoed among us. Without warning, two kids ran by us in a blur.

One of the boys yelled, "It's a taping tornado!"

They start running in circles around Barney and me, one running under the arm of the other as they crossed paths. Before we knew it, Barney and I were taped together, high and low. It happened so quickly; I couldn't fight it. I thrust my arms and legs out, but couldn't move them.

In a flash, the tornado was gone, leaving only Barney and me in a wake of destruction and a whole bunch of staring students.

"This is awesome," I said, not meaning it one bit.

"I like hanging out with you, too, man," the Barn Door said.

I chose not to respond to his optimism. "How do we get out of this?" I asked.

I tried to force my arms out, but they barely moved. The tornado hand wound us too tight.

"Whoa, dude! Stop struggling! We're gonna tip!" Barney yelled.

It was too late. Our upper body movement was too much for our base, which we couldn't move to steady our joint selves. We fell over like a giant Jenga tower. Thankfully, the duct tape kept all of our pieces from blasting in every which way, but still, it hurt.

And it wasn't over. As I looked past the knees and ankles of the kids gawking and laughing at us, I saw the unwelcome, shiny shoes of my nemesis approaching.

I took a deep breath and looked up Principal Buthaire's nose. It wasn't by design. It just happened that way.

Principal Butt Hair shook his head at me, seemingly with some pity.

"It must be difficult for you, Misterrrr Davenport, being on the receiving end of such a heinous prank. Maybe you'll learn your lesson. I doubt it, but I have a little bit of hope. Who did this to you?"

"I don't know who they were," I said. "They were different kids than last time."

"I'm not letting you out until you tell me."

"You can't do that." I didn't know who they were, but I was gonna find out. I really didn't want to get duct taped to people and/or architectural structures for the rest of my high school career.

6

Cheeks cut us free. Again. Principal Buthaire wrote out the familiar detention slips, as I tore the last piece of duct tape off me. I looked down at my clothes. I had that familiar and stylish glue-look circling my outfit.

I looked at Principal Buthaire. "Kinda reminds me of my prison costume that I wore to school. Remember that?"

"Yeah, those were the days," he said, sarcastically.

It probably wasn't the best thing to bring up, being that I wore the costume in protest for his prison-like rules, but I'm not known for having a solid filter.

I looked at Cheeks and couldn't help but ask, "They call you Cheeks?"

"Yep."

"Any particular reason?"

"None that I'm gonna share."

"That's fair," I said. "Thanks for the help. I think we're gonna be great friends."

"Let's hope not," Cheeks said, walking away.

I grabbed the detention slip that Principal Buthaire was

holding out for me with a smile. It wasn't worth it to argue about it. I just had to figure out a way to avoid getting duct taped every day. Who knew that would ever be an issue?

Barn Door and I headed down the hall to class. His optimistic spirit was seemingly at a low point.

"Why does this always happen to me? Are we going to get detention every day? These are the first two detentions of my entire life."

"It's not you. It's us." It wasn't the best answer, but at least he knew he wasn't alone.

"How can we stop this?"

"I don't know. They're different kids every day. Different techniques. We'll have to keep thinking."

"Okay. See you later," Barn Door said, turning down the west wing.

"Toodles," I said, and headed off to class.

I made my way to science and walked in late again. Miss Kelvin stopped her lecture and looked at me as I entered.

"Sorry. I kinda got tied up," I said.

"Like literally," Martin said. "Look, the dork has a duct tape tail."

Half the class laughed. I tried to look behind me to see, but I couldn't. I felt my butt and eventually tore off the tape. Thankfully, it wasn't too attached. The last thing I needed would be to tear my pants off by accident. I wasn't even wearing my Batman underwear, which at least would've gotten me cool points. Or maybe not.

Miss Kelvin said, "That's enough class. We're going to do our first lab today, so why don't you head back to the lab tables."

I walked to the back of the room and slumped into my seat next to Flea.

"Hey, Austin. Don't worry about that clown. I'll pummel him with dodge balls during gym class in your honor."

"Thanks."

"Normally, I charge for that, but since you're helping me in science, consider it on the house."

"That's very nice of you."

"Last night, I was reading some of the stuff you recommended, and I had a question."

"Really?"

"Yep. It's really important."

"Okay," I said. I wasn't sure what was so important about chemical elements.

"Are farts on the periodic table?"

"Sort of. It's not its own element, but a fart is made up of a handful of different elements on the periodic table. Nitrogen, Hydrogen, Methane, carbon dioxide, and oxygen." Yes, I've studied the chemical make-up of farts. I'm a middle school science genius. What else would I study?

"Dude, that's amazing."

"You know what else is cool? Each person probably has a different chemical makeup, but those are the key elements."

"Farts are like snowflakes? OMG. This is awesome. Oh, test mine!" Flea let a fart rip that rattled the metal chair. Half the class stared over in our direction. We were a great pair.

"I don't have a fart tester on me," I said, breathing through my mouth.

"That's unfortunate. I wish I had known that earlier," Flea said, seriously.

"Me, too."

"But still. That's so cool! Science is awesome!"

"Well, not everything in science relates that closely to farts. I don't want to get your hopes up."

"What about burps?" Flea asked, eagerly.

"They have the same elements, minus the butt bacteria."

"You are rocking my world, little man."

"Happy to be of service."

"This could be the year I graduate! Who knew that the answer was a middle school genius?"

"Did you go to Cherry Avenue Middle School?" I asked.

"Yep. Great place. The best five years of my life."

"Do you happen to know Max Mulvihill?" I was asking about the bathroom attendant at our middle school. It's a long story.

"Absolutely. I usually skipped science class and napped there on the futon. It kept me fresh."

I didn't want to say that it probably also kept him in middle school for an extra two years.

"Does Max have a satellite location here?"

"Nah, man. There's only one Max. I miss that dude."

I WAS IN BETWEEN PERIODS, about to head to lunch. I was throwing my junk into my locker when my favorite someone, Randy, slid up beside me with his signature smirk painted across his face. I wondered if it ever came off.

"Davenfart, I haven't heard anything about you getting signatures for the election," he said, shaking his head. "I can't believe you're not gonna run against me. I've finally broken you. You don't even try anymore because you know you can't win. It's sad, really. If I ever respected anything about you, and it was only a tiny bit, it was that you had fight. You were totally overconfident, but you had guts, which is more than I can say for most of these duds around here. But now you don't even have that."

I could feel my blood starting to heat up, but I knew he was just trying to get under my skin to make me run. I took a deep breath and forced a smile. "If you ever played fair, I might consider it. But I'm just gonna enjoy watching my girlfriend trounce you. It will be fun to watch you crumble under the pressure of losing to a girl." I didn't care one bit about what gender, color, or religion someone was. Randy didn't like to lose to anyone, but I knew it would hurt him even more if it was a girl. And Sophie would make it even worse. She was the first girl he liked when he moved here, and she chose me instead. She's a very intelligent young woman, which is just one of the many reasons why I knew she would make a great president of the eighth-grade class.

"I'm going to crush her. Is she ready to ride the pain train? 'Cause it's leavin' the station. Woot woot!" Randy said, walking away.

"I think it's more like putz, putz!" I called after him, as I shut my locker.

7

I was with my crew at lunch. Despite the horrific food, it was the best part of my day. I got forty-three minutes with Sophie and my friends. I slipped into my seat next to Sophie and grabbed my spork. I couldn't wait to dig into my toxic tofu.

"Signatures are starting to happen," Cheryl said.

"Who's getting signatures?" Sophie asked.

"Randy, of course. He was boasting in history class that he hit his goal by second period," Cheryl said.

"I heard Lyla Reese is looking for signatures," Ben added.

"I haven't heard of anyone else," Sammie said.

"Lyla Reese. She could be tough," Cheryl said. "She's smart, motivated, and outgoing."

"And not afraid of a cat fight," Luke added, laughing.

Ben joined in. "She literally wrestled a cat at Russell Gate's fifth grade graduation party."

"Who won?" Sophie asked.

"The cat," I said. "She played connect the dots with Lyla's freckles. Still, she's fearless."

"Well, I only need a few more signatures," Sophie said, smiling. "I barely had to ask anyone and I could've gotten it done last period, but I wanted you guys to finish it off." She handed the sheet to Sammie.

Sammie, Ben, and then Luke signed it.

"Last but not least," I said, taking the sheet from Luke.

"Thanks, guys," Sophie said. She took a bite of her soup and said, "We need a salad bar."

"Oooh, I love raspberry vinaigrette," Ben said.

"Anything is better than this," Luke said, pointing to his soup.

"I'm not sure this toxic tofu is better than anything," I said.

"Two words. Reuben. Chowder," Luke said. How do you take a great sandwich and turn it into a soup?"

"You can't go back from sandwich to soup. It's an inferior nutritional delivery mechanism," I said, annoyed. "How dare they?"

"How many soups do you know that have been turned into a sandwich?" Sammie asked.

"That's not the point," Ben said. "Everybody knows that sandwiches are better than soup."

"I can see you feel very strongly about this," Sophie said to Ben.

"I might run for president over this," Ben said.

"I thought you said the election was a sham?" Sammie asked.

"Yeah, my grandma said dead people vote."

"Like ghosts?" Luke asked.

"Yeah, I think that's what she meant," Ben said.

"This is like a school election, though. Do ghosts care about middle school elections?" Cheryl asked.

"I don't think she meant ghosts. But people pretending to be someone else," Sophie said.

"Oh, so cheaters," Ben said, his face lighting up.

"I don't think anyone will cheat," Luke said.

"Have you met Randy or seen the people running this place?" I asked.

"How are we supposed to guard against dead people voting?" Sammie asked.

"I have a speech to write. We'll worry about voting zombies another time," Sophie said. She looked at me and asked, "Do you want to go with me to drop off the signatures?"

"Sure," I said.

We dropped our trays off and headed to the main office. I had a big question to ask her.

"So..." I stalled. "I know we talked about it last year, but never did anything about it. Can I move into your locker?"

"Sure," Sophie said.

"Great. I have less time to get settled now that I'm in high school and all."

"Mr. Big Shot...Just kidding."

This was a big step. Lesser couples had broken up over the locker move in. My idiot brother, Derek, stressed over it the year prior.

We entered the main office, all smiles. Sophie stepped up to Mrs. Murphy at the front desk.

"Good morning, Mrs. Murphy. I wanted to hand in my signatures for the class election," Sophie said, confidently.

"Thank you, dear," Mrs. Murphy said.

"Who else is in?" Sophie asked, more tentatively.

"Umm, Randy Warblemacher. He's such a doll," Mrs. Murphy said, gushing. "Lyla Reese and Zack Newton. I think there's only one more signature sheet out there, unless

Dr. D. has more. I don't know who that last sign in sheet is for."

"Thanks," Sophie said.

"Good luck, sweetie."

As we left the office, Sophie said, "Okay. This is manageable. Who is Zack Newton?"

"He's kinda quiet. I don't really know too much about him. He's the dark horse of this election."

"What does that even mean?" Sophie asked.

"I'm not really sure what the connection is between politics and equines."

"Mr. High School using big words like equine."

I chuckled. "Oh, yeah. I'm real big time. I've been incapacitated by duct tape three times this week."

8

I t was time. All of the signature sheets had been turned in. We sat in the auditorium, waiting for the eighth-grade presidential candidates to be announced in front of the entire grade.

Sophie sat in an aisle seat. I was next to her with Ben to my right and the rest of the crew down the row from there. The front half of the auditorium was filled with eighth graders. The crowd was buzzing. Dr. Dinkledorf, our history teacher, strode out on to the stage wearing a fake beard and an Abe Lincoln-like top hat. There were a lot of strange looks and a few laughs as he stopped in front of the podium and disconnected the microphone from the stand. Ms. Pierre stood off to the side of the stage, watching.

Randy yelled, "You gonna do magic tricks, old man?" Randy was usually a huge suck up to teachers, but because Dr. Dinkledorf was old, like really old, he gave him a hard time because the poor guy couldn't hear anything.

"Yes, Teddy Roosevelt said, 'Speak Softly and carry a big stick!'" The kids laughed. Dr. Dinkledorf said, "Welcome! It's time to announce our candidates for the eighth-grade presidency. When I announce your name, please join me on the stage. Randolph Warblemacher."

Randy stood his annoying self up to cheers from across the auditorium. He smirked the whole way up to the stage and took his place next to Dr. Dinkledorf.

"Lyla Reese."

Lyla walked up stage to a smattering of applause.

"Zack Newton."

Sophie leaned over and whispered, "I wonder who the final candidate is."

I shrugged as Zack met the other candidates on the stage.

"Sophie Rodriguez."

Sophie stood up. I joined her and clapped the entire time she walked up to the stage. She got about the same amount of cheering as Randy.

"And our final candidate is Austin Davenport! Come on up here, Austin!"

I didn't move. I leaned over to Ben and asked, "Who'd they say? Kinda sounded like me."

"It was," Ben said, shocked.

"Austin, come on up here!" Dr. Dinkledorf said again.

I made eye contact with Sophie, which was a bad idea. The lasers nearly melted my brain. My stomach was in knots. I had no idea what was going on.

9

My chest was thumping. My mouth was dry. I looked over at my friends. Ben and Sammie were confused. Cheryl looked like she was going to throw me into a Camel Clutch, the most deadly wrestling move ever designed.

I shrugged at them and said, "I didn't sign up."

There were a smattering of applause and boos. And a whole lot of confusion.

"Why is he running against his girlfriend?"

"Why is she dating him in the first place?"

"Who's going to vote for him?"

I was less than excited. I looked up onto the stage as I walked down the aisle toward the stairs. Dr. Dinkledorf was fussing with his fake beard, oblivious to the treacherous situation I was in with Sophie. Ms. Pierre was actually smiling. What the heck was going on? Why would she want me to run? Unless she was going to karate chop me in half in front of the entire crowd and this election was just a big ruse to get me up on stage before I died.

My dread level rose with each step up to the stage.

Sophie's lasers continued to burn into me. My stomach was twisted like a giant Twizzler. Before Sophie dumped me on stage in front of the entire eighth grade, I decided to straighten things out with Dr. Dinkledorf.

I stopped in front of him and whispered, "Sir, I didn't sign up to run. I don't even want to run."

Dr. Dinkledorf frowned. Had I not been in panic mode, I probably wouldn't have been able to take him seriously.

"Really? That doesn't make any sense. I have your signatures right here." Dr. Dinkledorf waved me over to the podium. He looked out to the crowd and said, "Sorry folks. We'll be with you in a minute." Confusion spread throughout the auditorium.

Dr. Dinkledorf continued, "Let me see." He pulled out a folder and then handed me a slip of paper.

I scanned the list of signatures. I knew some of the people on the list. Nobody that stood out as being particularly devious. My name was hand written on the top. It wasn't my hand writing.

Before I could make any real sense of the whole thing, Ms. Pierre appeared behind us. I hadn't even heard her footsteps. It was growing more and more likely that she was a ninja. I was willing to bet on it. I nearly jumped out of my skin when I heard her voice ask, "What's going on here?"

Signature pages flew everywhere. The crowd laughed. I picked up the scattered pages while Dr. Dinkledorf and Ms. Pierre spoke.

Dr. Dinkledorf said, "He didn't submit any signatures and doesn't want to run."

"Well, he has to." She looked at me and said, "You're in. You need to see it through. I already sent the names to the printer for the ballots."

I handed the signature sheets to Dr. Dinkledorf and

asked, "Can't you change it? I'm sure they haven't printed it out just yet."

"Oh, they're very prompt," Ms. Pierre said, firmly.

"Can't you cross it off or tell the students not to vote for me?"

Ms. Pierre chuckled. "Oh, wouldn't you like that? As soon as I tell them not to vote for you, they're all going to vote for you. I see what you're doing here. You're trickier than I thought, Misterrrr Davenport."

"I'm not trying to trick anyone. I'm telling you I didn't sign up and I don't want to run. Even if I get every vote in the school, I have no interest in being president."

"You would make a good one," Dr. Dinkledorf said.

Ms. Pierre's face indicated she did not agree.

I said, "Sophie would make a better one."

Dr. Dinkledorf shrugged. "Sorry, Austin. The principal has spoken. You'll do fine." He patted me on the shoulder.

"I don't want to do fine."

"Have a seat so we can get on with this," Ms. Pierre said, faking cheeriness.

I shook my head as I slumped over to my seat. Sophie was still fuming mad. I thought I saw smoke coming from her ears.

"What did you do?" Sophie asked through gritted teeth.

"I didn't do anything. I didn't sign up."

"Then what happened?"

"I don't know." I looked at Randy. He smirked. "I know. I know it all."

"Now's not the time to be an arrogant jerk."

"I'm not. I meant that I know who did it. Randy signed me up."

Before we could continue the conversation, Dr. Dinkledorf continued the presentation. I wasn't broken up about it.

"Here are your five presidential candidates!"

The crowd cheered. A chant started. "Ran-dee! Ran-dee!"

"That's enough," Dr. Dinkledorf said. The crowd settled down. "I urge you to get to know each candidate and what they stand for. They will be preparing speeches and their platforms over the weekend. We will have another assembly on Monday for them to present to you their ideas. This is not a popularity contest. This is about voting for the right person to lead our eighth-grade class."

Another "Ran-dee!" chant broke out, seemingly failing to take Dr. Dinkledorf's message to heart.

"Thank you for your attendance and may the best candidate win," Dr. Dinkledorf said, tipping his oversized top hat to the crowd.

~

IT WAS LUNCH TIME. I sat with my crew in the cafeteria, mesmerized by the mysterious meatballs that sat in the tray before me. "Is this an optical illusion or are they really moving?"

"This is no time to joke, Austin," Sophie said, angrily. "You've really messed this up."

I wasn't sure if Sophie would add this item to her platform, but she was better than anyone at getting mad at me for things that weren't my fault.

"I didn't sign up. I don't know how many times I have to say it. Randy signed me up. He wants to beat me. He enjoys it. I think it's his favorite hobby." I looked at Sophie and asked, "Why would I want to take votes away from you?"

"You think you'll take votes away from me?" Sophie asked, annoyed.

"Some people do like me. And we have the same friends. Jeesh. No need to jump down my throat."

"Sorry. My competitive side is amping up."

"Hadn't noticed," I said, sarcastically.

"Why would he risk the chance that you could beat him?" Cheryl asked. "It's not like you haven't beaten him at things before."

I shrugged. "Maybe he wants to try to split our vote. Maybe he was scared that Sophie would crush him. This way, he can win and enjoy his favorite hobby."

"He totally Goblet of Fired you," Ben said, referring to the time when someone entered Harry Potter in the Triwizard tournament, hoping that he would blow himself up.

"He did. I just can't stand how badly he cheats at everything."

"So, what do we do now?" Sammie asked.

"I'm not gonna run. No posters. No speeches. No nothing. I won't even get one vote. Unless my girlfriend wants to vote for me."

Sophie shook her head. "Nope."

"That's fair," I said, shrugging. "I'm gonna try again to get out of this thing."

~

I WENT to see Dr. Dinkledorf before my next class. I know he already deferred to Ms. Pierre's ruling, but surely, he didn't want to make a mockery of the election process. I entered his classroom with a few other kids. Dr. Dinkledorf was going through his lecture notes. Fortunately, he wasn't wearing the fake beard and hat anymore.

Dr. Dinkledorf looked up at me. "Austin, my boy! To what do I owe the pleasure?"

"I don't want to run. I'm not going to participate in any way. It's not fair. I didn't sign up."

"Sometimes, those are the people who make the best leaders. The people have spoken. They want you to run."

"I don't think that's the case here. I think someone added me to split the vote." I kinda knew it was Randy and I thought if I could prove it, then they would have to let me out of running and leave me off the ballot. "I didn't put the signatures in. Who handed my sheet in?"

"Nobody handed any of them to me. They all went to the main office. You should probably ask Mrs. Murphy, although it doesn't matter at this point. Ms. Pierre already said you're on the ballot."

"Even if I could prove voter fraud?"

"I'm not sure nominating someone to run is voter fraud.

Class is about to start," Dr. Dinkledorf said, nodding at the near-full classroom. "Do you need a late pass?"

"Please," I said, dejected. I took the pass and said, "Thanks."

"Have a great day!" Dr. Dinkledorf said.

I was nowhere near as excited as he was. I sulked my way to my next class. As I headed toward the East wing, I stopped dead in my tracks. I saw plastic and duct tape, my new nemesis. I really didn't have room for another nemesis in my life, but there it was. The east wing was sealed up. I hadn't been down that way since school started. I forgot about the announcement that it was closed down for construction.

I backtracked and took a different route to my next class. On my way, I ran into Zorch. He was scraping gum off a locker. It looked like riveting work.

As I approached, Zorch looked over at me and said, "Hey, buddy. How are you?"

"Been better. What's going on in the east wing?" I didn't know if I should ask what happened to Max, my friend and bathroom attendant. It's a long story.

"Asbestos," Zorch said, simply.

"What the heck is that?"

"Bad stuff."

"Is it safe now?"

"It's safe until they start tearing it down."

"How does that make any sense? Why would they tear it down then?"

"I don't know. Some of it is exposed, I guess. They're supposed to start in a few weeks. It's the oldest wing we have. It was the first school house when our town was just starting out."

"When is it gonna be fixed?" I asked. I couldn't imagine

middle school without Max. He was always there to give me some advice or a snack when I couldn't bear to finish the cafeteria's attempt at food.

"I don't know. They were supposed to do it over the summer, or at least get started, but the construction firm got backed up. Typical."

I didn't want to ask about Max straight out. I always assumed that Zorch was getting some sort of cut from Max's operation. I mean, how else would someone be able to run a private bathroom service inside a public school bathroom? "What about that bathroom? It's very convenient."

Zorch tried to hold in a smile, but didn't do a very good job of it. "It's in the process of being shut down until the wing is reopened."

"Thanks. Well, I'll see you later."

"Okay, buddy."

I continued on to my class, thinking about Max and the bathroom. Where would he go while the wing was shut down? Travel the world? Write a novel? Join the Peace Corps? I had to talk to Max before he was gone. I looked down at my late pass and turned around.

I headed back to the east wing. I stopped at the corner and stared at a piece of loose duct tape. I slapped it for good measure. I was due a victory. I looked around to make sure there weren't any ninja principals lurking in the shadows. There were none, at least that I could see. Or couldn't see.

I pulled back the plastic and the duct tape, squeezing extra hard, and slipped behind it. I walked to the bathroom door and pushed it open.

"Zorch?" Max called out.

"Nope. It's me, Austin," I said, walking in. "I knew Zorch knew about this place!"

"Oh, hey. How else did you think I could run this place here?"

"It makes sense."

"What's up? Why are you here?" Max asked, curiously.

I looked around the bathroom. It looked like a regular public school bathroom. No foosball tables, refrigerators, hot tubs, or artisanal cheeses. It was sad. "I saw that the wing was closed. I wanted to see where you were headed."

"Still trying to figure it out. Any ideas?"

"A safari? Surfing in Hawaii? Or there's the high school."

"High school? You mean open up over there?" Max asked, intrigued.

"That's exactly what I mean. They could use your services. A lot of kids have jobs, so they have extra income to spend. Some of them were your previous customers so you've already built a brand with them."

"Hmm. I hadn't thought of that. Cheeks might be a tough sell."

"Do you know why they call him Cheeks? Anything to do with butt cheeks?"

"Don't know," Max said, seemingly distracted.

"I think it could be big for you," I said. And I could still see Max. Maybe he would stay there for my entire high school career.

"Well, if I figure it out, you poop for free, my man."

I was moving up in the world. I just didn't want to move up too far. I still had to figure out how not to be president. True, it was a big jump to go from free pooping at Max's to class president, but it wasn't as big as you might think.

10

L ater in the day, I saw Randy already busy at work on his new campaign. As I walked through the Atrium between periods, a few pockets of kids had gathered to socialize before the next class. I wanted to hear what nonsense he was spewing. I used my best ninja skills to slip into the group beside him, undetected.

Randy stood talking to a kid I didn't know and said, "Yeah, man. I can do that for you. If the photo club needs new lighting, the photo club gets new lighting. You don't need it for my head shots, but some of these clowns around here need all the help they can get, you know what I'm saying?...Speaking of clowns- It's Austin Davenfart, ladies and gentlemen."

I guess my ninja skills were less than I had hoped for. I was a little bit surprised. I stepped toward Randy and said, "I did almost join the circus once."

"You should probably keep that to yourself." Randy looked over at the photo club kid and said, "Yo, I'll see you later." The photo club kid walked away, eyes darting in all directions.

"For once, we're in agreement. I couldn't help but hear you making promises that I'm sure you won't deliver on, so I figured while we're on the subject, why did you sign me up for the election?"

Randy stepped toward me and laughed. "I didn't do it. But I'm happy that somebody did. Now I can trounce you. You're a loser. You exist so I can win." He patted me on the shoulder.

Anger rose up inside me. I didn't even know what to say, which was out of the ordinary for me. Even if it was stupid, words usually came out.

Randy didn't wait for me to respond. "I've got work to do. The Italian Culture Club is gonna host a family style fundraiser for me on Friday night."

"In exchange for what?" I asked.

"Never you mind, Davenfart."

I was livid. Randy walked away, smirking. I couldn't believe that Randy didn't sign me up. It wouldn't be the first time that he wasn't responsible for something like this. It could've been my brother, Ms. Pierre, or even Principal Buthaire, for all I knew. Or Randy could've been lying. He had his tenth-degree black belt in lying. I had to figure it out.

After my next class, I stopped into the main office. Mrs. Murphy looked up from her papers as I approached her desk.

"Austin, I don't recall Ms. Pierre wanting to see you."

"I just have a question about the election. Did you take in all the signatures?"

"Yes."

"I didn't sign up. Do you know who put mine in?"

"I don't know. I think it was left on my desk when I got back from a break. I thought you just chucked it there because you didn't want to get ninja-starred by Ms. Pierre."

You know your principal has a problem when the staff openly discusses her weaponry with the students.

Mrs. Murphy continued, "Don't worry. She's not here. She's meeting with a donor who is going to sponsor the east wing when it reopens."

"Okay. Thanks. I guess."

～

I COULDN'T WAIT for the day to be over. I sat in eighth period, counting the seconds. Just Charles sat beside me, taking furious notes. I looked down at my own notes and all I had was, 'Randy stinks.' I made an additional note to borrow Just Charles' notes.

With two minutes left of school, the Speaker of Doom crackled. Ms. Pierre's voice echoed into our classroom, "Good afternoon, everyone. It's a new year and my first full year here at wonderful Cherry Avenue. We are going to make some enhancements. You've probably heard about our east wing upgrade. The great news is that it will be named in my honor for all that I have achieved since arriving here."

"What has she achieved?" Just Charles asked.

"She strikes fear in the hearts of students, so there's that," I said.

"A very generous donation has been made by a parent of one of our students. Grayson Storm and his technology firm, Storm Cloud, are big supporters of the great work we do here. You can read more about it in Monday morning's Gopher Gazette. In the spirit of enhancements, I have a few additional things that I'd like to upgrade."

"Here we go," I said.

Ms. Pierre continued, "From this moment forward, detention will be known as 'after-school character enhancement', the cafeteria as 'the five-star food emporium', the nurse's office will be 'the student health and wellness center', guidance will be 'the neural and emotional enrichment center', and the gymnasium will now be 'the mind, body, and spirit spa and retreat.'"

"Oh, yes. Dodgeball, it's good for the soul," I said.

"It scars my soul," Just Charles said.

The last bell of the day rang, signaling an end to the day's misery, if you don't count the homework that went along with the day. We picked up Sophie on the way to the Atrium.

"Hey," I said.

"Hi there," Sophie said to Just Charles and me. She grabbed my hand as we walked down the hall. It was her way of saying 'sorry' without actually saying it.

"What do you think of all that?" Just Charles asked.

"I don't care what they call stuff. I don't like Regan's dad making donations to the school. It's only gonna give her more power. She's intent on turning Cherry Avenue into Regantown."

"The Pretty Posse. What a joke," I said.

Just Charles added, "She's recruiting an army. She gets more and more followers every period, it seems. All of them are carbon copies of her."

Regan was right by the door of the Atrium as we entered. She air kissed Ditzy Dayna and said, "Best friends 4 eva!"

"Ugh. What has society come to?" Sophie said to us.

Regan looked over at us as we passed. "Oh, look who it is. The losing election candidates. Lahoo Zaher. That's Swahili for loser, and you are losers."

"Yeah, I'm pretty certain that's not true," I said.

"Oh, you speak Swahili, now?"

"Let's not be ridiculous. I don't and I'm pretty certain you don't, either."

"We'll just see about that," Regan said, walking away, her pouty-lipped posse on her heals.

"That doesn't make any sense," Sophie said.

"Welcome to middle school," Just Charles said.

"I don't get this whole posse thing," I said. "Jasmine Jane, not surprising. Peyton Pruit, not losing anyone. Ditzy Dayna? What is she doing?"

"I don't know." Sophie said. "She's avoiding me. Regan has some sort of power over these girls."

IT WAS FOOTBALL SEASON. Oh, joy. My parents dragged me to another one of Derek's games that Saturday morning. At least Sophie and Ben joined me. We could make fun of Randy and my brother, at least when my parents weren't listening.

It was a home game at Cherry Avenue, a menacing place for opposing teams to play. The stands were packed with Gopher pride. The fearsome Bisons were squaring off against our squad. Despite our Gopher name, our team was quite good. We would've made the state championships the year before had I not stolen Grimmwolf the Gopher, our savage mascot, which, in turn, stole the team's mojo. As I looked around the stands, I hoped people didn't still hold it against me. I had admitted to the whole thing.

The game was tight. Neither team seemed to be able to put the other away. It was late in the fourth quarter and it was tied, 14-14. We had the ball only fifteen yards out, threatening to score. Randy, our quarterback, lined up

behind the center. Derek and Nick DeRozan set up behind
Randy.

"What are you thinking? 44 Blast?" my dad asked.

I was actually thinking that it would be nice if Randy got
run over by a herd of angry Bison, but I didn't think I should
make that known. "Yep. It could work."

Randy looked to his left and then to his right as he
assessed the Bison defense. His mouthpieced voice called
out a muffled, "Blue forty two. Blue forty two. I wear polka
dots and pink stripes!"

The center hiked the ball. Randy turned and faked the
handoff to Nick as the 44 Blast was designed. Derek ran to
the ball. Randy held it out for Derek to take, but pulled it
back and took off running the other way. Half the Bisons
pounced on Derek, expecting him to have the ball. For once,

I wished I had played football and was able to pummel Derek like that.

The crowd cheered as Randy sprinted to the sideline, dodging would-be tacklers. Half the team was still laying on top of Derek, thinking they had made the tackle. Randy had sprinted past most of the others. Only one player remained between Randy and the goal line. The Bison player rushed toward Randy, his head down. Randy jumped as the player lunged for Randy's legs. The crowd held its breath as Randy soared over the defensive player and then erupted into cheers as Randy's feet touched down for a touchdown in the end zone.

The Gopher squad engulfed Randy in hugs. He broke away from the pack and held the ball above his head as he ran to the sidelines. The cheerleaders were jumping and kicking like wild as Randy approached. I saw Regan hand out three signs to some of the cheerleaders, keeping one for herself.

Regan popped up, holding a sign that read, 'Randy.' Amy Geller's read, '4.' Monica Carter and Ditza Dayna pressed their two signs together that read, 'Presi-dent!'

Sammie stopped mid cheer and looked up at the sign. She scowled at Ditzy Dayna and walked off the track to the grass, away from the rest of the group.

"That's not fair," Ben said.

"We gotta get serious. They're not messing around," Sophie said.

"Frank's Pizza at my house tonight?" I said.

"I'm in. We need to work on my speech."

"Me, too. Let's do this," Ben said. "I'm sure Just Charles and Cheryl will come, too."

"Let's just hope that Evil Chuck doesn't show up." He wasn't the best house guest, although secretly, I did enjoy some of his antics.

11

The leaders of Nerd Nation were fully assembled at my house. My basement had become Sophie's campaign headquarters. We were scattered about on the couch and a few bean bag chairs, chowing on Frank's, the best bread, cheese, and sauce around. The guy was a culinary artiste.

Cheryl, who was Sophie's campaign manager said, "The first order of business is figuring out what to do with Austin. A vote for Austin is a vote not cast for Sophie."

"Should I even participate in anything? Maybe I should just pretend that I'm not even running. I won't give a speech. I'll skip the debate."

Ben said, "Maybe you should just go up there and say, 'I stink. I have nothing to say. Don't vote for me. Thank you.'"

Just Charles said, "You could even add, 'I'm a loser.'"

"Yeah, well, the stink and loser parts might be a little aggressive, but yeah." I thought for a moment. "But maybe I should make a real speech."

Sophie looked at me like she was going to kill me.

I added some clarification. "To help you. I'll tell

everyone why they should vote for Sophie. It could be like having two speeches for Sophie, while everyone else gets one. I can make fun of Randy."

"I don't know if her base is gonna go for that," Cheryl said.

"My base?" Sophie asked.

"Your voter base. You need to appeal to girls and single boys."

"Wait, what? Single what?" I asked. Nobody said anything about appealing to single boys.

Cheryl continued without acknowledging my concern, "Lyla can definitely win the nerdy boy vote if you don't make them happy."

"Hey, I'm the only nerdy boy she wants to make happy."

Ben chimed in, "It's all about popularity. Just make up a bunch of stuff that you're gonna give them. We can tell everyone you're an orphan. We can put you in crutches."

"The pity vote. I like it," Just Charles said, pounding a soda. "How many pity votes do you think are out there?" he asked Cheryl.

"Sophie is not a pity-vote candidate. She's a powerful, young woman who will lead with strength."

"Here, here!" I said, raising my soda can.

We all clinked our cans. And, of course, Just Charles took a huge swig.

"Slow down, buddy. Evil Chuck wasn't invited," I said. He was an emergency kind of guest only.

"I think I do like the idea of Austin giving a speech about how good Sophie will be as President. You don't have to bash yourself. I think it will be much more powerful for him to be pro-Sophie than anti-Austin."

"Thank God. I'll do it, if it's what you want," I said to Sophie.

"Thanks. If I wasn't running, you know I would vote for you," she said.

"Me, too," Sammie, Just Charles, and Cheryl said, together.

I looked at Ben.

"What? Oh, yeah. Me, too."

"Real convincing," I said, laughing.

We worked on Sophie's speech all night. We were reasonably pleased with it. Sophie was going to practice it on Sunday, and we would assemble for the actual speech on Monday. We didn't get a chance to write my speech. I was going to write it the next day.

IT WAS MONDAY MORNING. We had assembled at the assembly for the presidential candidates' first speeches. There would be a debate a few days later and then a final speech just before Election Day.

I stood backstage with Sophie. Lyla and Zack were there, too, both practicing their speeches off in the distance. Sophie paced in a circle mouthing the words to her speech and practicing her hand gestures.

She was more nervous than I had ever seen her. I was going to tell her to picture everybody in their underwear, but that would've just been plain weird with Dr. Dinkledorf and other teachers in the room. Honestly, picturing anyone in their underwear is probably a bad idea. Not sure why people always say to do that when giving a speech. I would think it would be pretty awkward.

"Just take a breath. You're gonna do great."

Sophie said, "I want it so bad. I'm afraid I'll mess up. I'm afraid they won't like me."

"Just be yourself. You're awesome. Everybody knows it."

Randy's speech was starting. I walked to the edge of the stage, just behind the curtains.

"I don't want to watch," Sophie said, pacing. "Just tell me how he does."

"Okay," I said, peeking through the curtains.

Randy stepped up to the podium. "Greetings, fellow Gophers and Americans. My name is, well you already know my name. But for mind-washing-er branding purposes, I am Randy Warblemacher. You may know me as the star athlete, leading the football, basketball, and baseball teams, or perhaps you saw me star in the lead role of our holiday musical."

Some people in the crowd cheered while others booed. I wanted to join in on the boos, but being that I was on the stage and a fake candidate, I didn't think it was presidential.

Randy continued, "I'm just spit-balling here, but you may have also seen me take home the science fair trophy, and I'm dating Regan Storm. Do I need to say more? I don't, but I will. I never miss an opportunity in the spotlight."

Hearing Randy's speech made me wonder if this was what Calvin Conklin was like growing up. Calvin Conklin was our local newscaster, whose arrogance rivaled Randy's, but his intelligence did not.

"Or perhaps you've seen me at one of my concerts as the lead singer of Love Puddle."

Somebody yelled, "Love Puddle stinks!"

Randy ignored it. "I have a three-point platform. No homework, no detention, no pop quizzes!"

The crowd erupted into cheers.

"Vote Randy Warblemacher on Election Day!"

Randy walked off the stage waving to the crowd and pointing to people in the front of the auditorium. He actually looked like a politician, flashing his smile in his suit and slicked-back hair.

He thrust his fist into the air and yelled, "U.S.A.! U.S.A.!"

The crowd joined him in the chant. Most people rose to their feet clapping and cheering as Randy left the stage.

"Beat that, Davenfart," Randy said, smirking.

Sophie walked over to me, ignoring Randy.

Randy looked at her and said, "Good luck, Mrs. Davenfart," and headed off stage.

Lyla walked past us. She primped her hair, straightened her suit jacket, and took a deep breath.

Dr. Dinkledorf announced, "Next up, we have Lyla Reese!"

Lyla strode confidently to the podium, to a smattering of applause.

Lyla cleared her throat and scanned the crowd. She looked like she might puke, but then she smiled and said, "Thank you everyone for all the support and well wishes you've given me these past few days. I'm excited to be your next President. I ran because you asked me to. No, needed me to. You needed a voice. And I am that voice. As your President, I will get funds to give each student a new laptop, which will be allowed in class. We will upgrade our technology to the 21st century with smart boards and those cool Japanese toilets that clean themselves."

I saw Zorch standing on the side of the auditorium and his face morphed white.

Lyla continued, "Gum chewing will be allowed in class. If they want us to act like adults, they should treat us like adults."

Zorch fell to his knees and wobbled there for a moment. I thought he might pass out. The thought of scraping hundreds of pieces of gum off the desks, walls, and floor was too much for any custodian to handle, even the best like Zorch.

"I will fight for open book tests, because in the real world, we have Wikipedia!"

All the nerds groaned. Studying was their one advantage. Well, ours.

"Why do we have to memorize everything? It's just a waste of creative brain space. And finally, I will push for free ice cream in the cafeteria! Vote Reese if you please!"

The place erupted into cheers. It was a strong speech. She appealed to the nerds with all the technology and the non-nerds with open book tests. And then there was the ice cream, which doesn't need explaining.

"We don't have a good slogan," I said.

"How about 'Davenfart supports the arts'?" Randy quipped.

I turned around and shook my head, and then turned back toward the stage without saying a word.

As Lyla passed, she looked at Sophie and me and said, "I'm gonna drop you like a toilet seat."

"A Japanese one?" I asked.

"They drop themselves, idiot."

Sophie looked at me and said, "I can't believe you didn't know that, High School."

I chuckled. "I just started high school, so I don't know everything." I was happy she was cracking jokes. It was better than cracking under the pressure.

Zack Newton walked past us, white as a ghost. He tried to stretch the wrinkles out of his t-shirt, which had a giant question mark on the front.

There were a few claps as he was announced. Zack stepped to the podium. He adjusted the microphone a little higher with a shaky hand.

"My name is Zack Newton. I don't believe in making campaign promises. My competitors are going to make a lot of promises, most of which they won't deliver on. So, I'm not going to make any promises. I just want to say that I'm the best man for the job. I've been asked what my platform is. You'll have to vote me in to find out!"

"You're up, Soph," I said. "Good luck. I know you'll do great."

Sophie took a deep breath and cracked her neck on both sides. That was the Sophie I knew. Ready to crush it.

Dr. Dinkledorf said, "And now we have Sophie Rodriguez!"

Randy called out from the back, "Go get 'em, Mrs. Davenfart!"

"Don't listen to him. You got this."

Sophie walked out to the podium, not looking at the cheering crowd. She adjusted the microphone down. She looked over at me. I gave her a thumbs up.

"Good morning. My name is Sophie Davenfa, er Rodriguez." Some people laughed, but she continued, "I love being a student at Cherry Avenue. It's been a great experience so far. And I think it can be even better. We need healthier food options. How are we supposed to be our best when we have to eat the seafood surprise? I mean, we don't even know what's in it. I will fight for better food. We also need more activities for kids who don't play sports. I will fight for more funding for school clubs, art programs, and the theatre."

Mrs. Funderbunk, our music teacher and theatre director, yelled, "Mrs. Funderbunk is voting for you!" She always refers to herself in the third person. You get used to it.

"I'm not saying sports aren't important, but we act like

everything else is not. My name is Sophie Rodriguez and I'm the candidate that cares!"

Sophie walked off the stage to cheers. She didn't look overly enthused.

"That was bad," Sophie said, shaking her head.

"No, it was great. You slipped up at the beginning, but you recovered nicely, and got a lot of applause."

"You think so?"

"Definitely."

"Next up is Austin Davenport!" Dr. Dinkledorf announced.

"Davenfart, your shoe is untied," Randy said.

"Yeah, right. Like I'm gonna fall for that," I said.

"Nice try, Randy," Sophie added.

I walked out to more cheers than I had been expecting. I waved to the crowd. I didn't often get good attention in school. And then I had to go and ruin it all. Apparently, my shoe really was untied. I stepped on my laces of my left foot, causing me to trip. My body propelled forward, hurdling toward the podium. I twisted my body to avoid a head-on collision. I crashed into the podium, my shoulder smashing into its upper half, both it and me, smashing to the ground with a smack. I wasn't sure if it was the wooden podium or my ribs.

Gasps and laughter burst throughout the auditorium. My shoulder was throbbing, which was surprising because I thought most of my blood had rushed to my embarrassed face.

I could hear Randy's high-pitched laughter over the crowd.

Mr. Muscalini was the only one who had anything positive to say. He called out, "Nice tackle, Davenport!"

Dr. Dinkledorf rushed over to me and helped me up.

"You okay?" he asked.

"Fabulous," I said, dusting myself off.

"Do you need a minute?" Dr. Dinkledorf said.

"No. I'll just get started."

"Let me stand the podium up. If you'll help this old man."

"Just leave it. It doesn't look like it'll even stand up."

I walked over to the microphone, which was dangling only inches above the floor, and disconnected it from the stand. I walked around to the front of the podium and sat down on it. I wasn't sure if it would crumble to pieces or even disintegrate into dust, but thankfully, it didn't. My ego didn't have the strength for it.

A bunch of people cheered as I was about to begin. I felt butterflies swirling in my stomach and a hammer pounding my shoulder. I got nervous when I spoke in front of people before I started, but was fine once I began. I'd given two big speeches in front of the board of education, plus I was the lead singer of Mayhem Mad Men. If I could sing in front of thousands of people, I was pretty certain I could sit and talk in front of a few hundred. Although, when it's all of your friends and potential future ridiculers, it does amp the tension up a notch.

I held the microphone to my mouth and said, "That's one way to make an entrance."

The crowd laughed. I continued, "I didn't sign up to run for president of the eighth grade class. It was a ploy by one of the other candidates, either because he..." I paused as I looked at Randy on the side of the stage. "...takes pleasure in beating me at things or worse, because he wanted to split the vote among a lot of different candidates so that the best candidate, Sophie Rodriguez, wouldn't win. I don't want to be your president. I'm not the best choice. Sophie Rodriguez is my choice and she should be yours. For president. Not as your girlfriend."

The crowd laughed again.

"I'm not going to participate in the debates or give another speech. You're in great hands with Sophie Rodriguez. She should be your eighth-grade president. Just don't hold her hand. Thank you for your time. I'm going to the student health and wellness center. I think my arm is gonna fall off."

More laughs. "And oh," I said, leaning down to tie my shoe. "I should probably take care of this."

I finished tying my shoe and walked off the stage to loud cheers. When I got to the side of the stage, the other candidates were all gone, except for Sophie.

She rubbed my shoulder and asked, "Are you okay?"

"I think so," I said. "How did I do?"

"I think you missed your calling on the Gopher football team," Sophie said, laughing.

"Yeah, right. Or maybe they'll vote me in as class clown."

I followed Sophie through the guts of the auditorium. As we walked out the back of the auditorium into the hallway, students were heading in every direction. The first person we saw was Lionel Lamar, a surfer dude, who I became friendly with during the Cupid's Cutest Couple Contest. You might remember that debacle.

Anyway, Lionel clapped me on my definitely-broken shoulder and said, "Dude, you're the man, taking down the man. You're flouting the system. You're a flouterer."

I preferred to be called a floutist, but I wasn't going to argue.

"You just spit in the face of the man," Lionel continued. "Knocking down the podium was so symbolic, man. You were taking down THE man. The authority that rules over us in this place, dude."

"What do you mean?" I asked. I really had no idea what he was talking about.

"You just don't care, man. That's gonna get you a lot of votes, dude."

"I don't want votes," I said. "I clearly told everyone that Sophie was the best candidate."

"Yeah, just keep doin' that, bro, and you're gonna punch your ticket to the presidency. Later, dude!"

I scratched my head. I wasn't sure if I just didn't understand what was happening or if I was having an identity crisis- was I a dude or a man?

Sophie was less confused and more angry. "That didn't go well."

"It's only one person and we know he's a little out there. Let's not get all worked up just yet. We'll see how Cheryl's polling data comes back. She said she expected to have a quick one done by lunch."

THERE WERE two surprises at lunch. The first one was the daily surprise that was the actual meal. We never knew what was truly in it or how our tiny bodies would react to the concoction of inferior ingredients. The second surprise was the polling data.

Cheryl Van Snoogle-Something entered the cafeteria a few minutes after we sat down with our trays. She strode over to us quickly.

Sophie looked over at Cheryl and said, "It doesn't look good. If she's not happy, I'm not gonna be happy."

Cheryl slipped into the seat across from Sophie and looked directly at her. "A bunch of us at the Gopher Gazette plan to poll the eighth graders throughout the campaigning process. It will be helpful to us."

"What's the deal?" Sammie asked.

"We have some work to do, but I'm confident we can get there."

"How bad is it?" Sophie asked.

"You're in third, but it's really close."

"I'm guessing Randy is in the lead, with all of his ridiculous promises and bone-headed followers. I mean, it should be a two-candidate race with Sophie. But I guess Lyla's in second with her laptop and ice cream combo?"

"Nope," Cheryl said, looking at me. "You're in second place."

Ahhh, farts.

12

I t took me a moment to recover. I almost threw up my lunch, which could've been just a coincidence. Once I felt the urge not to hurl, I looked at Cheryl and asked, "Me? How is this even possible? I fell flat on my face in front of the entire class. Why do people even want to vote for me when I don't want to run?"

"Because you're the nerd of nerds," Ben said. "You're not better looking than anyone, your clothes barely fit half the time. You're barely average among the average."

I took a deep breath, waiting for my soul to recover. "Thanks for laying that out so helpfully. I'm going to talk to the school psychologist. For a friend. What is it even called now? The neural and emotional center for distressed youth?"

"You're likable," Cheryl said. "And Ben's right. You're one of us. And you've shown over time that you are not afraid to stand up to authority."

"Well, I don't want to be likable anymore. I'm gonna be the worst candidate they've ever seen. I'm gonna show everyone why they should never vote for me."

"I can get behind that campaign," Luke said.

"Thanks. I think you could be very helpful in helping me screw this whole thing up."

"That's what I do best."

"If I can tank, Sophie will take her rightful place ahead of Randy."

At least I hoped that would be the case. I didn't want to be the one to cause Sophie to lose. Granted, it would really be Randy's fault. I mean, when is it not? But still, it could be a relationship crusher, and I didn't want that.

THE CAMPAIGNING WAS off to a quick start and Randy Warblemacher was leading the way. As I walked through the Atrium with Sophie on the way to fifth period, there were already campaign posters up on the walls.

Regan, or the Queen of Mean, as we had started calling her, stood with her Pretty Posse. They were looking up at a poster of Randy scoring the touchdown from Saturday's game. He was leaping over the last defender on the way into the end zone.

"There's the Chick Clique," I said. "Now they even worship posters of Randy?"

"It's the Pretty Posse," Sophie said.

"I think my name is better," I said.

"What does the poster say?"

In big letters, the top of the poster read, 'Winners win' and at the bottom, beneath the picture, 'Randy will win for you.'

"Randy only wins for himself," Sophie spat.

We were only about ten feet from the Pretty Posse when Ditzy Dayna broke away from the pack.

Sophie smiled for the first time all day and said, "Hey, Dayna! What's up? I haven't seen you in a while."

Regan snapped her fingers and said, "Let's prance, Posse."

Dayna ignored Sophie, and fell in line behind the Queen of Mean as they strutted out of the Atrium.

I looked over at Sophie. Tears welled up in her eyes. She tried to hide it by looking away, but it was too late.

"Are you okay?" I asked, stupidly. It was obvious that she was not okay.

Sophie put her head on my shoulder. "Why is she being so mean? She was a good friend."

"I don't know. I will talk to her."

∾

I WAS able to catch up with Ditzy Dayna the next morning

before history class. I was surprised that she even talked to me. I walked back to her desk with about two minutes before the bell rang.

"Hey, Dayna," I said. "What's going on with Sophie? When you were with Regan yesterday, you ignored her."

"I'm afraid of Regan. Plus, she's really cool."

"And that's more important than a real friend? Sophie cried when you ignored her."

"I don't know," Dayna said, staring at her desk.

"You think Regan is a real friend?" I whispered, as kids started to fill the room. "The same girl you're afraid of?"

"She told me you wouldn't understand."

"I don't, because I would never have done that to you."

"We barely know each other, Alvin."

I shook my head and walked away. In her defense, she didn't have much of a brain.

History was pretty boring. Even though Dr. Dinkledorf was pretty animated and excited about each lesson, learning about the American Colonies for the fifth time was less than interesting. Instead of paying attention, I planned out my campaign to tank in the election. I pretty much had no idea what to do. I thought that maybe if I could get our ex-Principal, Butt Hair, to endorse me, it could cause my candidacy to spiral into the toilet. And I'm not talking about one of those fancy Japanese toilets. But other than that, I didn't really have any ideas. And I was pretty certain that I would not be endorsed by Butt Hair.

I moped into lunch. I didn't have any good answers for Sophie on the direction of my campaign nor would should be happy with my conversation with Ditza Dayna.

I stared into my tray of cubed beef and mashed potatoes, wondering what the cafeteria staff could've done to actually mess it up. For once, it didn't actually look like poop.

When Sophie sat down with her tray, I decided to get the Dayna thing out of the way. I said, "I talked to Dayna."

"What did she say?" Sophie asked, angrily.

Ben asked, "What happened?"

"Long story," I said. I looked at Sophie and said, "I don't really have a good answer for you. She thinks Regan is cool and is also scared of her. I think that she's afraid that if she isn't in the Pretty Posse, I still think Chick Clique is better, that she'll be treated like garbage like they do to everyone else."

Sophie was on the verge of tears again. She nodded, not saying anything.

"She'll come around," I said. "My sister had the same problems. Eventually, Dayna will see Regan for who she is."

"But then there's Jasmine Jane and Francesca Marino and Tonya Watkins."

"They're ignoring you, too?" Sammie asked.

"No. Worse. They keep making snooty comments and whispering about me while laughing and staring in my direction. I'm sick of it. What did I do to deserve any of this?"

"You don't deserve it at all," Ben added. "None of us do."

And then I got her mind off her problem. I wish it had been through a different tactic, but it worked. I took a scoop of mashed potatoes. I felt something that was not overly mashed. I thought it was a piece of potato, so I bit down on it. Big mistake. I don't know what it was, but I bit into something that crunched like a car running over a soda can.

"Ahhh, farts!" I yelled, grabbing my cheek. "What the heck was that?"

"What happened?" Sophie asked.

"My mashed potatoes crunched. I don't think that's supposed to happen. I think you're onto something with improving the food, Soph. But we'll talk more after I go to the dentist."

"Are you okay?" Sophie and Cheryl asked.

"I think so, but if things go poorly at the dentist, maybe I can make a campaign video for you without any of my teeth."

Cheryl said, "We want you to keep a low profile. No videos. If you lose all your teeth, you could get the pity vote."

"I was kidding."

"Seriously, though. What do we have that we can use?" Cheryl asked.

"Sophie has a great slogan," I said.

"The candidate who cares," Sophie said, smiling.

"We need poster ideas," Cheryl said. "Did you see Randy's garbage on the wall?"

"Yep," I said. "I've got a good poster idea. How about we make a poster with Yoda on it, but with Sophie's face that says, 'Vote for me, you will.' We can Jedi mind trick you into the presidency." It was probably not the best of ideas.

"I don't need the Jedi mind trick to win!" Sophie said, a little too loud.

"That's not the tactic you're looking for. I get it," I said.

We didn't really make any progress on Sophie's campaign, but my campaign was apparently hard at work. And not my own toilet-tanking campaign. Somebody was running a positive campaign for me. Yeah, for real.

I walked with Sophie, Sammie, and Ben through the Atrium on our way to fifth period when my face caught my eye. Yes, a strange thing to happen, I agree. But it did. I glanced over at Randy's football poster and saw a second one next to it with my face on it!

"What the..." I said, intelligently. I broke off from my crew and started walking toward the poster in question.

At first, I thought it was a poster meant to humiliate me, which was Randy's specialty, but it wasn't. It was a poster of me rocking out at Battle of the Bands. I looked pretty good, leather pants and all. The poster read, 'Vote Austin Davenport! Mayhem Mad Men's lead singer should be your leader, too!'

My crew fell in behind me, all staring up at the same mysterious poster.

"This is how you're gonna tank?" Sophie asked, annoyed.

"I didn't do this," I said. "This reeks of Randy. It's too much like the football one."

"Somebody is running a counter campaign," Sammie said.

"A counter campaign for the election I'm trying to lose?" I asked, confused.

I was living in the bizarro world. Randy wasn't trying to tear me down. He was building me up. I could only assume it was to tear me down at some point, but it was pretty weird, nonetheless.

"We have a problem," I said.

"You're gonna win this election," Sophie said, monotone.

13

A fter the last bell, I hung out with Sophie, Ben, Cheryl and Just Charles in the Atrium before the buses took off. We were plotting Sophie's campaign strategy out, and the best we had so far, was a poster with her holding a basket of fruit with the saying, 'Vote Sophie. Eat healthy.'

Randy hustled through the Atrium, presumably on his way to football practice, with Regan and her Pretty Posse in tow. Ditza Dayna, Jasmine Jane, and four other girls had gathered. Cheryl hopped out of our pack and into Randy's path. I wasn't sure what was going on. I thought she might tackle him.

"Randy, the Gopher Gazette would like to interview you about the upcoming election."

Randy stopped. Regan and the Pretty Posse followed his lead.

"No way, Cheryl Van Snoogle-Something. Why would I do that?"

"Because you can lay out your platform for the voting public."

"But you're Sophie's campaign manager. I'm not stupid. You'll be biased," Randy scoffed.

"I have something called journalistic integrity. And another journalist can interview you."

"I don't think so," Randy said.

Cheryl stepped in front of him again. "Look at it this way. I can trash you either way. I don't have to interview you."

Randy thought about it for a moment, but Regan stepped in front of him. She threw her hair back, hitting Randy in the face, and said, "Pass."

"Okay. If that's how you want it," Cheryl said, annoyed.

Regan smirked and said, "Girls?"

All the girls repeated, "Pass." They threw their hair back over their shoulders, pushed out their pouty lips, and followed the queen bee out of the Atrium.

"I don't even know how to respond," I said.

"Has that ever happened to you before?" Just Charles asked.

"Buses are coming," Sophie said. "Everybody meeting up at Austin's tonight?" She looked at me and asked, "Can we do something other than pizza?"

My heart sank. My life no longer had meaning. The things that used to give me joy filled my heart with meh.

Ben asked, "Dude, you okay?"

"Did. You. Hear. What. She. Said?"

Sophie laughed, which was welcome, given that it hadn't happened too often in recent days. "It's just pizza. How about Burger Boys?"

Burger Boys was my second favorite restaurant behind Frank's Pizza. My life force returned to my body and all was good again in the world. Well, besides my epic battle with

Randy and the campaign that I was trying to lose, but kicking butt in.

"I think we can do that. I think the Burger Boys will do a great job preparing you for the debate."

THAT NIGHT, the Burger Boys did us right. And our crew hit the spot, too. We were at campaign headquarters in my basement, which smelled fantastically like bacon. Sophie, Cheryl, Ben, Just Charles, and I outlined every campaign issue that each candidate had with Sophie's position on it, along with ideas and one liners on how to respond to the other candidate's issues and put it into a giant book.

"So, if I'm Lyla and I say that I'm gonna give free laptops to everyone and toilets that wipe your butt, which I'm not sold on, by the way, you say what?" I asked.

"Can we make this more real and have Austin wear a wig? For Sophie's sake," Ben said.

Everyone laughed. "Yeah, for Sophie's sake. Right," I said, chuckling.

Sophie asked, "How are you gonna pay for all that *free* stuff?"

"I'll get the funds," I said.

"How? Our parents are gonna pay higher taxes for toilets that wipe our butts?"

"Oh, that's good," Just Charles said.

"Try another one," Cheryl said.

"I draw the line at pretending to be Randy," I said.

"I'll do it," Ben said. He looked at Sophie and said in his most arrogant voice, "No more pop quizzes!

"How are you going to get rid of pop quizzes, Randy? The teachers aren't going to change how they grade us just because you don't want to take tests. You're just promising all this stuff to win votes."

"This book is gold. I love this thing. I'm gonna memorize and practice every possible scenario and response. This is the key. Thanks, everyone," Sophie said, smiling.

SOPHIE'S CONFIDENCE was quickly shattered, however. The next day, I ran into her on the way to lunch. Her jaw was clenched as she power walked through the hallway. I sped up to catch her.

"What's wrong?" I asked with a furrowed brow.

"The book is missing," Sophie said, exasperated.

"What book?"

"*The* book. For the debate."

"Oh, no."

"You didn't take it?"

"I haven't been to your locker yet today. How could somebody have taken it? Did you make sure to lock it this morning?"

"I think so," Sophie said, rubbing her chin.

"Does anybody else know your combo? How did they even know it was in there?" I asked.

"No and I don't know," Sophie said, wiping a tear away.

Mr. Muscalini strode through the hallway, his wide shoulders nearly brushing up against the lockers on both sides of him. He looked down at Sophie and stopped abruptly.

"What's going on here? There are no tears allowed in my gym."

I said, "We're not in your gym and isn't it a spa now, sir?"

"Do you have a death wish, Davenport?"

"No, sir," I said, my voice shaking. I took a step back, awaiting his response.

"I like mud masks, whirlpools, champagne, and gossip as much as the next guy, but my gym ain't no spa or spiritual retreat. It's all about the blood, sweat, and tears! You got that?"

"Actually, no," Sophie said, scratching her head. "I think we're both confused."

"Yeah, you said no tears in the gym and then that gym was all about tears," I said.

"That's right, Davenport!" Mr. Muscalini yelled, and walked away without clarification.

I looked at Sophie and said firmly, "I'll get it back." I had no idea how, but my confidence at least made her smile. I was crying on the inside, though.

AFTER LUNCH, I entered the Atrium to cut across to my next class. Of course, election mayhem was ensuing. Jace Thompson, a seventh-grade journalist on the Gopher Gazette, was standing on one of the benches with an ancient bull horn. Cheryl must've given Randy a good idea. He needed a guy inside the paper to help spread his message.

I was pretty certain that bull-horning was against school policy, but, of course, Ms. Pierre was nowhere to be found when someone other than me was breaking the rules.

The bullhorn echoed, "Vote Randy Warblemacher! Do the other candidates have celebrity endorsements? Of course, they don't. But Randy just received an endorsement from front-man Rider Dane of 64 Farts! Rider loves Randy's no-homework policy. A vote for Randy means no homework!"

I just shook my head as I passed. It was getting ridiculous and I was still pretty upset about the book. We had worked hard on that and it would give Sophie's opponents an unfair advantage. True, none of them seemed to have much substance, but Randy was a master of slights and insults, so I was sure he would figure out a way to use it against her or us.

I wondered if I should confront Randy about the book

or turn him in to Ms. Pierre. I figured that if I confronted him, it would just make it harder to get it back, as he would know we were onto him and Ms. Pierre would probably do nothing. Had it been me who stole the book, I'm sure the S.W.A.T. Team would've been called and maybe even a ninja street gang from Chinatown.

There was only one option as far as I was concerned. Do nothing. Just kidding. I was going to have to steal it back. If Randy was gonna take it home, he would have to have it with him in the gym locker room during practice. That's where I would strike.

I really didn't have much of a plan, other than hoping Randy was arrogant enough to leave his locker unlocked. Zorch was a good buddy of mine and usually willing to help, but I was pretty certain he wouldn't give me the keys to break in and take stuff from other kids' lockers.

After the buses left for the day, and all the sports teams had headed out to the fields, I slipped into the boys' locker room. If anybody asked, I was going to be grabbing my dirty gym clothes and heading to the robotics club.

I knew exactly where Randy's locker was. Everybody in our gym class did. His obnoxiousness echoed throughout the room every other day during eighth period. I stood in front of his locker, the padlock staring back at me, locked iron tight. I didn't know what to do.

I heard voices coming. I was about to run for the door, but I tripped over a backpack on the floor. After that, there was only one way to exit and that's where those voices were coming from. I quickly jumped up onto the bench and dove across to the top of the lockers. My gut slammed into the top edge of the lockers, knocking the wind out of me. I kicked, scraped, and clawed my way up to the top and rolled away from the edge. I wasn't sure if I was hidden, but it was better than just standing there, fiddling with Randy's locker.

Is it possible to pull every muscle in the human body? Because I think my crazy spy move might've done that to me. I lay on my back with my head turned to the side, trying to see what was going on.

Randy, Nick, Kevin Dudley, Derek, and my brother's friend, Jayden, entered, smacking each other and horsing around like idiots do. I hoped it would be enough to keep them from looking up at me. What were they doing back inside?

Randy's, Nick's, and Kevin's lockers faced me, which kept me hidden, but Derek and Jayden were on the opposite side, so it was an easier angle for them to see me.

The jock jerks spun the dials on their padlocks and opened their lockers.

"These things are so annoying," Jayden said, grabbing his cup out of his locker.

"And they taste gross, too," Derek said, taking his cup and trying to press it over Jayden's mouth and nose.

It boggled my mind why girls always wanted to go out with them.

"Dude! Knock it off," Jayden said, fending off Derek's cup attack.

Derek stopped and shut his locker. And then it happened. Nick flicked Derek's ear. Derek turned around, ready to return the brutal attack. You may think I'm exaggerating, but you haven't seen how big Nick is. He reached over toward Nick and then stopped dead in his tracks. Confusion spread across Derek's face as he looked into mine. He looked like he was about to say something. I quickly put my finger in front of my mouth in a shushing position.

Derek shut his mouth. For once. I wasn't sure why. My

only thought was that he disliked Randy more than he disliked me.

"Hey, man. Get this bag outta here. I almost broke my neck," Randy said.

Without warning, Nick tossed something up over top of the lockers. There was nothing I could do as it soared above me, hovered over me for a quick second, and then plummeted down to me, crushing the family jewels. I bit my finger, which kept me from yelling or maybe even crying.

I held my breath, hoping that I didn't give myself away.

"What's in that bag?" Randy asked Nick DeRozan.

"What are those things with all the pages in them?"

"Books, idiot?"

"I didn't know books were short for books, idiot."

"Ugh. If there were books in there, why didn't it bang when the bag landed?" Randy asked, annoyed.

"They're used to being quiet in the library?" Nick said, scratching his head

The crew all started laughing.

"Seems weird, though, right?" Randy asked. "Why didn't it?"

That was my cue to exit. I slithered to the other side of the lockers and gently placed Nick's bag down next to me. I looked down into the empty row of lockers. I was a good seven feet off the floor. I went into ninja stealth mode. And promptly fell off the lockers and landed on the floor with a heap and a crack of broken ribs, or was it my skull?

"What the heck was that?" Randy asked.

Derek said, "I'll check it out."

"Thanks, Davenport. You can never be too careful during election season."

I lay there on the floor, struggling to get to my knees. Derek turned the corner. He stood over me and literally kicked my butt. Not hard, but still. Nobody likes to get their butt kicked. I looked up at him.

Derek mouthed, "Go." He turned around and went back to the other side of the lockers.

"Just some junk from on top of the lockers. Must've fallen when somebody closed a locker or maybe a delayed reaction from Nick's feathery books."

I held my ribs as I slipped out of the locker room, unsuccessfully. Well, I was successful in slipping out of the locker room. I was an epic failure at stealing the book back.

14

The debate was rapidly approaching. It was only a day away. Sophie was still freaked out about losing the book. Thankfully, we had our own copy saved on Just Charles' laptop, but all our takedowns and comebacks were in Randy's hands.

I was down in campaign headquarters waiting for my friends to arrive. I had to figure out how to neutralize the book. I missed my shot at getting it back. And it was a pretty bad shot. How could I get the advantage back? I lay on the couch, staring up at the ceiling, talking to myself.

"How can I counter Randy's counters? I don't think I can. I wish I could blow up the book. I don't even know where it is. I should just make sure the debate doesn't happen."

I'd taken down school dances before, why not a debate?

"But how? What am I good at? Science. Burping the alphabet. Not sure how that's useful. At least related to the debates. Hmm. I'm a fabulous singer. Again, not useful here. Mayhem. I'm good at creating mayhem. True, sometimes I don't mean it. How can I create mayhem?"

I thought for a few minutes without any ideas. I was starting to get frustrated.

"Mayhem. Mayhem. Mayhem. Mayhem," I said, faster and faster.

I grabbed a baseball Derek had left on the floor next to the couch. I tossed it from hand to hand. For the first time, playing sports, if you want to call it that, paid off for me. Well, first I nearly knocked myself out as the ball hit off the tip of my finger, bounced off the couch and conked me on the head.

"Oww!" I said. "Only I could conk myself on the head like that. Well, most of my friends could too. Conk! Conklin! Calvin is the answer!"

I took out my phone and looked Calvin up on social media. I wrote, 'So excited that Calvin is gonna moderate the debates at Cherry Avenue Middle School tomorrow night!'

'I am?' was Calvin's response. 'Will there be cameras there?'

'Absolutely! Have Ted call Ms. Pierre for the details!'

'I wanna do it, but I just had surgery! I'll try!'

I wasn't sure if it would work, but it was worth a shot. Calvin would neutralize the book in no time. If he showed up.

WE HAD another brainstorming session at my house. Sophie, Just Charles, and Cheryl Van Snoogle-Something were over. We were back to fueling ourselves with Frank's Pizza.

My father came down the basement stairs carrying two glorious, steaming pizza pies.

"Do you guys think that you can get Frank to donate pizza to the campaign? I'm going broke here," my dad said, laughing.

"Sorry, Mr. Davenport," Sophie said, sheepishly.

"Just kidding, sweetheart. We're happy to support you."

Just Charles said, "Thanks for the pie, Mr. D."

"No problem," he said, placing the pie on the table and heading back upstairs.

I opened the first box and inhaled the spectacular Mac 'n Cheese pizza. I doled out the slices and then sunk my teeth into my own slice.

"Why don't they outsource all the cafeteria's food preparation to Frank?" I asked.

"I wish," Sophie said.

Cheryl got us back on track. "I've analyzed the race. There's only one athlete candidate. He's going to get those votes plus most of the shallow, popular kid votes."

Just Charles added, "Randy's campaign strategy is to capture those votes plus spread around the remaining votes as much as he can to the rest of the candidates, so he can win."

"And laugh when I lose," I said. "He's generating support for me, to take votes away from Sophie."

Of course, the arrival of pizza meant that Derek was not too far behind. He lumbered down the stairs and over to us.

"What a surprise," I said.

"You owe me," Derek said. "I saved your butt in the locker room."

"You did." I was pretty certain that he was still in a major deficit of owing me stuff after all the torment he had given me over the years, but I swallowed the rest of my pizza and then my pride and said, "Thanks for that."

"What the heck were you doing up there?"

"I was trying to stick it to Randy or at least keep him from sticking it to us. He stole a book from Sophie."

"There's no trying to stick it to Randy. You either do it or you don't."

"Thanks, Yoda."

"I'm not Yoda."

"Yeah, you totally just paraphrased Yoda."

"I'm gonna paraphrase your brain," Derek said, tearing a slice from the remaining pie.

"You should. You might actually get good grades."

"Later, dorks," Derek said, heading back upstairs with two slices.

"Sorry for the idiotic interruption. We've got a debate to plan for," I said.

"What do we do about the book?" Sophie asked.

"We're still waiting to hear from Calvin and his crew. They said he had a conflict. Ted said he was getting a Brazilian butt lift or something," I said.

"What the heck is that?" Ben asked.

"I don't wanna know," Sophie said.

"So, there's not much we can do about it now," Cheryl said. "You're the only candidate who actually wants to accomplish real stuff. Just stick to that."

"Should we change it?" Sophie asked.

"Change what?" Cheryl asked.

"My platform. I mean, nobody likes me," Sophie said, shaking her head.

"Everybody likes you."

Sophie scratched her head. "What ideas will win? What will kids vote for?"

"They'll vote for all the stuff Randy and Lyla are promising, but can't deliver," I said.

"So, I should change it then. Nobody likes what I have to

say. Austin doesn't even want to run, and people want him to be president more than they do me."

"That's not true," I said.

"It is true," Sophie said, annoyed. "That's what the poll said."

"Polls are just a snap shot of one period of time," Cheryl said. "They can change in a heartbeat. Kids' opinions change more often than Luke changes his underwear."

"I can vouch for that," Just Charles said.

"How do you know how often he changes his underwear?" I asked.

Just Charles ignored me and said to Sophie, "I think you should stick to what you've said. They're good ideas. If you don't win, you don't win."

"Easy for you to say. You're not gonna lose. I can't even begin to imagine how much garbage I'll get from Regan and the Pretty Posse if I lose."

"Who cares what they think?" I asked.

"I do," Sophie said.

"Why?" Cheryl asked. "They're idiots."

"I don't know. And I don't know what to do. I'm gonna get creamed in the debates," Sophie said, holding her head in her hands.

15

The next morning, my bus was early, so instead of hanging out in science before the bell, I went to visit Max in his new high school digs. As I approached the door, there was a sign that said, 'Under Construction.' I wasn't sure if Max would even be there. I put my ear to the door, but didn't hear anything. I pushed the door open slowly.

"We're closed," Max's voice said.

"It's me, Austin," I said, slipping into the bathroom.

"Oh, hey Aus. Come, check this out. I'm really excited about my new concept."

I walked in and looked around the room. It was unreal. I don't know why I was always surprised when I saw Max's newest bathroom decor, but he always seemed one step ahead of me.

Max led me through the bathroom on a tour. "We're taking public school bathrooms to the next century. Japanese toilets that clean themselves, flat-panel TVs in the stalls. 5G. We're going to trounce the competition."

He was definitely right. The only thing the competition had to offer were those little, white pee tablets in the bottom of the urinals.

"I gotta start advertising soon," Max said. "I need revenue."

"What are you gonna do?"

"I might take an ad out in the Camel Chronicles. Obviously, I'm gonna get some social media buzz going. I'm sure I can get a video of the Japanese toilet flushing to go viral."

"Just make sure it hasn't been used first."

"Point taken." Max laughed.

And then I had a brilliant idea. "What if instead of having those pee tablets, you put a picture of Principal Butt Hair in the bottom of the urinal? Who wouldn't want to pee here?"

"Dude, you never cease to amaze me. You're going to be a brilliant business man one day."

"The feeling is mutual. You've got an amazing place here. I'm sure you'll do fantastic.

AFTER SCIENCE WAS OVER, I headed back to middle school. Jace Thompson and members of the Pretty Posse were handing out the newest edition of the Gopher Gazette.

Advisory was typically pretty boring, so some new reading material would be useful. I wasn't sure why they were so keen on handing them out in the Atrium. Usually, we got them in Advisory. I walked over to Jace, since I had no interest in dealing with any of the P.P. That's Pretty Posse for short. I felt it was an appropriate name for them. Anyway, Jace turned his back when he saw me coming.

I furrowed my brow, walked around in front of him, and held my hand out for a paper.

Jace speed-walked to Becky Feldman and called out to her, "Hey, Becky! Here's the copy you asked about."

It was weird, but I didn't think anything of it. I didn't care about reading it that much. It was too much effort for a nerd to start chasing people around the Atrium to get a newspaper.

I continued on to our squad's usual meeting place, under the dogwood tree. Sophie, Sammie, and Ben read the copy that Sophie was holding, while Cheryl and I both approached at the same time.

Sophie looked up at Cheryl. "This is unbelievable. You let them print this?"

"What is that?"

"What do you mean?" Sophie asked. "It's a copy of the Gopher Gazette. And it trashes me!"

"We don't have a publication coming out today. It's

supposed to be tomorrow after tonight's debate. Let me see that," Cheryl said, holding out her hand.

Sophie handed it to her with some 'tude.

Cheryl grabbed it and rubbed the paper. She said, "This isn't the paper we use. This is fake news." She read the first article aloud, "Sophie Rodriguez claims she wants healthier food options at Cherry Avenue Middle School, but the evidence suggests otherwise. She's been a student here for more than two years. Has she ever lodged a complaint with the school about its food service? Our investigative reporting team decided to find out."

"This is unbelievable," Sophie said. "He's sending his attack dogs after us."

Cheryl continued, "An unidentified source in the main office confirmed that Ms. Rodriguez has never made any formal or informal complaints about the food or any other school issues. Hardly the student advocate she claims to be. In addition, Miss Geller, the lead lunch lady in the cafeteria, had this to say, 'The students love our food. Who doesn't love a good mystery? Whether it's the seafood surprise, the mysterious meatballs, or the curious chicken, the kids love the challenge of figuring out what's in that day's nutritious meal.'"

"Is she kidding me?" I asked.

"It gets worse," Cheryl said, and then continued to read, "The Gopher Gazette cannot endorse Sophie Rodriguez. We hate to use the word fraud- that is for you to decide."

Sophie wiped a tear from her cheek. I put my arm around her.

"We all know it's not true," I said.

"But they don't!" Sophie yelled, pointing to all the students in the Atrium.

"Well, I'm going to do something about this," I said,

angrily. I took the paper from Cheryl and said, "I'm going to see Ms. Armpit Hair."

Cheryl grabbed the faux Gopher Gazette from a kid walking by.

"Hey," he said.

"It's fake news. Don't waste your time," Ben said.

Cheryl said, "I'm going to talk to Mrs. Conklin. We're going to have to respond to this."

I STORMED into the main office as the bell rang for the school day to begin. Carl Sheffield paced the floor in front of the Speaker of Doom, preparing for the morning announcements.

Mrs. Murphy looked up at me from her desk. "Good morn-"

I cut her off. "I need to see Ms. Pierre immediately. It's a matter of national security."

"National security?" Mrs. Murphy raised an eyebrow at me.

I didn't appreciate her suspicion. "Is presidential election fraud not a matter of national security?"

"Hold on," she said, rolling her eyes. She picked up her phone and dialed. "Ms. Pierre? Austin Davenport says he has a matter of national security to discuss with you."

I may have been embellishing a little bit, but I was half convinced Ms. Pierre was some sort of government agent and would be willing to meet with me based on those circumstances.

I added, "Also, journalistic integrity. We have a fake news debacle on our hands."

Mrs. Murphy rolled her eyes again. She hung up the phone. "Ms. Pierre will see you now."

I walked into Ms. Pierre's office. I called it The Armpit. Principal Buthaire's old office was The Butt Crack, so I thought it was pretty fitting. I immediately noticed that it was spotless. She didn't even have a copy of Ninjitsu for Principals lying around.

Ms. Pierre looked down her nose and over her reading glasses at me. "Sit down, Misterrrr Davenport. It's a serious matter to claim that it's a matter of national security."

"National security is also a serious matter," I countered.

"Indeed. To what do I owe the displeasure?"

I handed over the fake news article. "Randy Warblemacher's campaign has been handing these out this morning, pretending to be our esteemed newspaper. People rely on the Gopher Gazette for all the goings on at Cherry Avenue Middle School. It is a grave offense to betray the trust of the students here."

"You don't say?" Ms. Pierre said, skimming the article.

I wasn't sure if she agreed with me or not. I decided to press while she still seemed open to my side of things. "I think Randy should be removed from the election for voter fraud."

Ms. Pierre put the paper down on her desk and took off her glasses. "How do you know it was Randy?"

"He's the only one who would do it. He cheats at everything. I once saw him cheat at checkers to beat a ninety-year old man."

"What proof do you have?"

That pesky thing called proof. Randy was good at implementing his evil plans without leaving proof. "I don't have any, but who else-"

Ms. Pierre held up her hand, cutting me off. "Without

proof, I'm afraid there's nothing I can do. I agree with you. This is an important matter that we need to get the bottom of, but we can't go around accusing people before we have proof," she said, attempting to hold in a smile.

"Well, you should start the investigation with Jace Thompson. He was handing them out. Regan Storm, too."

It was probably the wrong name to throw out there, given that Regan's dad had just given the school a ton of money to sponsor the new east wing in Ms. Pierre's honor.

I decided to change course before the whole thing fizzled. "What about all the campaign promises Randy made in his campaign speech? Clearly those lies shouldn't be allowed."

"It's part of the process. There's nothing to say he can't accomplish those things. Is it a given that you or Ms. Rodriguez will accomplish your plans?"

I didn't actually have a plan. I didn't want one. But I figured that would only confuse the situation. "No, it's not," I said, defeated.

"Is that all?"

"I guess so."

"Okay, then.

I wasn't happy. I didn't really think she would kick Randy out of the election, but I also wasn't sure why everyone seemed to favor him so much. I mean, he was a total butt kisser, but surely, she could see he was an idiot. Right? Wrong.

16

The highly-anticipated showdown among the presidential candidates was upon us. It was show time. The five candidates had all assembled back stage in the auditorium. Dr. Dinkledorf and Mrs. Conklin were there as well. The students filed in as we all paced around, waiting for the debate to start. I was there more to support Sophie than to actually debate.

Sophie was circling near the curtain, whispering key points to herself when Randy walked up to us.

"Tie your shoes, dork," Randy said to me, laughing.

I had no plans to walk out onto the stage, but I checked anyway, just to be sure. They were tied in double knots, just like when I left the house.

"Very funny, Randy. If you don't succeed as a con man, you might want to take a shot as a stand-up comedian. I'm sure some of the idiots out there will laugh at your stupidity."

"You've got a big mouth for a little kid," Randy said, angrily.

"Boys," Dr. Dinkledorf said, hustling over to us. Well, as

fast as the old guy could hustle. "You can be competitive without being negative."

Randy shook his head and walked away.

"Thanks," I said to Dr. Dinkledorf.

"Sure thing. You guys are going to do great out there."

"I'm not going out there," I said.

"What? Are you nervous? You'll be fine," Dr. Dinkledorf said.

"No. I never wanted to run. I want Sophie to win."

"Okay," Dr. Dinkledorf said, shaking his head. He walked away, mumbling something to himself.

I looked at Sophie and asked, "Are you ready?"

"I hope so. I know he's gonna use the book against me," she said.

"He might know what you're gonna say, but it's better than anything he can say. I can't believe I want Calvin to show up."

But instead of Calvin arriving, Ms. Pierre whisked by, a huge smile on her face. "Exciting news coming our way!"

"News," I whispered to Sophie. "Calvin?"

Ms. Pierre walked over to Dr. Dinkledorf. They had a discussion that I couldn't hear, but he didn't look happy. Which made me happy.

Dr. Dinkledorf returned a few minutes later and said, "Okay, candidates gather around. Calvin is here to moderate the debates, so we're going to get started.

"Yes!" I yelled.

Dr. Dinkledorf frowned and continued, "At least one of us is excited. There are five podiums. I will announce you in a moment."

The candidates all bunched up by the side curtain, as Dr. Dinkledorf hobbled out onto the stage to a smattering of applause.

Calvin slipped in behind us and clapped Randy on the shoulder. "Yes, it's me, but don't get crazy about it."

We all turned around and looked at him with blank stares.

"I can give you an autograph if you want, but we're about to connect on a personal level. My signature isn't worth anywhere close to that. Believe me, I've checked. But, if you really want my autograph, I can make it happen. Anybody?"

"I'm good," Randy said.

"How about you, short stack?" Calvin asked me.

"I've already got an autographed picture of you framed on my wall," I said.

"Really? I mean, of course you do."

Dr. Dinkledorf's voice boomed over the speakers, "Are you ready to meet your presidential candidates? Let us first welcome to the stage, your moderator. He's the face of Channel 2 News. Please put your hands together for Calvin Conklin!"

Calvin grabbed Lyla by the shoulders. He looked like he was going to impart serious wisdom upon her. Instead, he said, "If you're gonna fart, you might want to do that now. Good luck." And then to the rest of us, "Hold your noses."

Calvin turned and headed out to the stage, waving to the cheering crowd.

"Oh, you're too kind. Too kind. Actually, I can't hear you. Give it up for me!"

"And now," Dr. Dinkledorf used his best announcer voice, "Please welcome to the stage your eighth-grade class presidential candidates!"

Randy pushed Zack forward onto the stage and then said, "Lyla, why don't you go."

She smiled and followed Zack, who was still stumbling toward the far podium. Randy, of course, walked toward and stopped in front of the center podium.

"Good luck," I said to Sophie. "I'm sure you'll do great."

"That makes one of us," she said, and then forced a smile. Sophie walked out and took the fourth podium position.

Calvin's voice boomed, as he sat in a desk on the stage

facing the candidates. "Welcome, citizens of Gopherville! It's that time again, where we get to vote for the President of the United States!"

Calvin pressed on his earpiece, talking to his producer/babysitter, Ted. "Why do you always have to rain on my parade? Maybe one of these kids could be the president of the United States someday. What do you think of that, Ted? Maybe not the Davenfart kid, but maybe that Randy kid. He kinda looks like me. Oh, right. The debates." Calvin looked up at the candidates and said, "Sorry about Ted. He's a real downer sometimes. So, Ted tells me that we have five candidates, one of them apparently very short." He pointed to the empty podium nearest me. "That's not gonna win him any votes."

The crowd laughed.

"Davenfart? Are you there?"

Sophie leaned into her microphone and said, "His name is Davenport and he's not here!"

"Probably for the best," Calvin said. He looked at the folder on his desk and flipped it open. "Here's a list of questions that Dr. Dinkledorf and Ted put together for you."

Oh, no. The Book was back in play.

Calvin lifted the folder and tossed it behind his head. They sprayed into the air and floated down to the ground.

The crowd laughed again while soul-crushing defeat registered across Dr. Dinkledorf's face. He walked off the stage and took his place beside me.

"This should go swimmingly," he said, sarcastically.

"We're going rogue, people," Calvin said. "We're going no-holds barred style here. Does anybody know what that means?"

I pumped my fist when he wasn't looking.

None of the candidates answered.

"Neither do I, but we're doin' it anyway." Calvin looked up at the candidates. "You'll each answer in turn or Amanda Gluskin will put you in the Camel Clutch. Starting with the blondie to my right. Layla."

"It's Lyla. Reese."

"Got it. Layla. How would you handle the school's body odor situation? I mean, this place is just downright rancid."

"Air fresheners around people's necks," Lyla answered. "It could be the next IT fashion trend."

"Interesting. And you, guy?" Calvin said, looking at Zack.

It was nice that Calvin had prepared so well for the debate.

"I'll tell you after I'm elected," Zack said. "I like to play things close to the vest."

"Oooh, I like that," Calvin said. "And you, Randy, my dear boy?"

"Free body spray for everyone!" Randy yelled to cheers.

"Excellent point. Sophie? Your take on the stank?"

"How about the students take showers?" Sophie said, like the rest of them were idiots, which was not necessarily wrong.

There was some laughter and a few boos. I'm not sure who would actually boo the idea that people should take showers, but it was middle school. My take was that Randy won that round, even though, I knew he would never get the district to pay for 'free' body spray.

Calvin continued, "Starting with the mystery man to my right. I've lost sleep over this question for quite some time. Bells? Really? Should we start and finish classes with whistles?"

"Absolutely!" Mr. Muscalini yelled from the back of the auditorium.

Zack didn't even answer, but Calvin said, "I like the enthusiasm. Randy?"

"Yes. Life is a sport. Nobody rings a bell to start a sporting match."

"Well said," Calvin responded.

"Not so. There's boxing," Sophie said, landing the first punch of the debate.

"So, where do you stand on the bell or whistle issue?"

"It depends on what kind of whistle," Sophie said.

"I think students should be able to come and go as they please," Lyla said.

The students cheered like crazy. Despite Sophie's retort to Randy, it was obvious that Lyla won that round.

"Should the ingredients of the seafood surprise be withheld from the student population?"

Randy didn't even wait for Calvin to choose him. He yelled, "Free pizza for everyone!"

Sophie interjected. "No. We have a cafeteria crisis. The quality of our food is disastrous. How can you expect the students to pay attention and achieve their full potential when we're breaking teeth on mashed potatoes and cubed beef?"

Zack said, "I think the seafood surprise should remain a mystery."

Layla answered, "I think the seafood should be sustainable. We need to protect our environment."

Calvin craned his neck in the empty podium's direction. "Austin? Care to participate?" He shrugged. "I guess he's the short, silent type."

Sophie was fidgeting as she awaited the next question. The stolen book hadn't hurt her, but the debate wasn't going overly well either, which wasn't too surprising, since Calvin was running the thing. The news station must've made some serious donations to the school for us to keep having that clown back. And this time, I was grateful.

I looked up at Dr. Dinkledorf and whispered, "I've lost all hope in the political process, sir."

"Welcome to adulthood, Austin," Dr. Dinkledorf said, sadly. "We're doomed."

"Final question of the night," Calvin said.

"Thank God," I said, perhaps a little too loud, because both Sophie and Randy looked in my direction. Sophie was less than enthused while Randy gave me his signature smirk.

Calvin continued, "Why do you want to be president of the eighth grade class?"

It was actually a good question. I was so shocked, I had nothing to say.

Sophie answered, "I want to make our school better. Cherry Avenue is a great place, but we can do more for our students."

Zack said, "I'm not gonna answer that. Not because I don't know, but to not answer is more mysterious." He raised an eyebrow for good measure.

Randy thrust both fists in the air and said, "Money and power!"

The crowd cheered. I wasn't sure why.

Lyla said, "Because this school needs a strong woman leading us and I am that strong woman."

Ms. Pierre looked like she took serious offense to that statement.

Randy chimed in and said, "Yeah, it's certainly not Sophie, the anti-fun candidate."

"I am not," Sophie said. "You just make promises that you have no ability to keep. No detentions. Free pizza. Free body spray. How are you going to pay for it all?" Sophie looked at the crowd. "He can't. He's just saying whatever he has to in order to win."

Randy looked out at the crowd and said, "See what I mean?"

The crowd laughed again. Sophie gritted her teeth, but didn't respond.

"You heard what she said before. She's going to force us to shower? Who does she think she is? We have enough parents telling us what to do. We don't need another annoying one."

I thought Sophie might charge Randy and throw him into the Camel Clutch. Randy was much bigger than Sophie was, but she could do anything if she was angry and determined enough. She knocked him down last year during Cupid's Cutest Couple Contest. Unfortunately, I was blindfolded at the time and missed the whole thing, but it sounded awesome. I kinda ruined it by kicking Sophie in the face and knocking her two front teeth out shortly after that, but still, I look back on that night with fondness.

"Austin? Are you back there, buddy?" Calvin asked. "Quiet fella. Certainly, didn't distinguish himself tonight."

And then Lyla put the icing on the cake, ending the debate with a massive sneeze. She almost knocked herself out on the podium, which would've been better than what actually happened. As her head narrowly avoided the podium by moving it the side, the crowd gasped and then nearly puked as Lyla blew a giant snot bubble out of her right nostril.

She stood up straight and looked at the audience laughing at her, and rushed off the stage, nearly knocking me over as her shoulder banged into mine.

The sneeze is right up there with the fart as one of the most powerful and disastrous forces of the universe. While the worst-case scenario of a sneeze is certainly less than a fart gone wrong, there's no underwear for the face to act as a buffer. It's just nose, world, and snot.

Lyla didn't just eke out a cute little sneeze. Something like that could possibly endear her to the voting public. I could just see some of the kids in the auditorium say, "Aww, isn't she cute? I'm gonna vote for her for president." Hey, people have based their decisions on a lot less substance. Have you seen some of the clowns running things these days? Anyway, it wasn't that kind of sneeze. It was more like the Sneeze of Doom. And it doomed her political career. Not just for middle school or even high school. It basically ruined her for her entire life. Slow motion video, gifs, and memes swarmed the Internet after that unfortunate event.

Dr. Dinkledorf rushed on the stage, seemingly hoping to end the debate without Calvin making a further mockery of the system and before any other types of bodily fluids made their way onto the stage. He stopped in front of the empty podium and said, "Thank you-"

Calvin cut him off. "Careful, Austin's back there. Isn't he? Is he invisible? Oh, my God. He's invisible!"

The crowd laughed. Dr. Dinkledorf shook his head and continued, "Thank you all for your attention. Please give a round of applause for our candidates!"

The crowd clapped and cheered. A "Ran-Dee!" chant started and grew louder as Randy thrust his fist in the air, as the candidates all walked off the stage.

Randy leaned over, putting his face in front of mine and said, "Crushed it, Davenfart! You're gonna lose."

I laughed and said, "That's what I'm trying to do. Why do you think I didn't go out there?"

"So, you wouldn't embarrass yourself?" Randy asked.

Sophie blew past both of us, so I left Randy in the dust, chasing after her.

THE RESULTS from the poll weren't what we were hoping for. Sophie and I gathered with Cheryl in the Atrium after school, as I was waiting for Ben to catch the bus.

"It's not good. We slipped a little bit. But the good news is that there's no way Lyla is coming back from what happened. She's only at 2%. So, you picked up some of the feminist vote, but you lost some independents to Randy and Austin."

"I'm still gaining votes?" I asked, surprised.

"Yeah, you got 5% more than last time. It turns out that by skipping the debates, you're eating into Randy's base as the cool candidate," Cheryl said.

"This is unbelievable," Sophie said, rubbing her face with her hands. "What are the numbers?"

"Randy is at 44%. Austin is at 26%. You're at 23%. Zack is at 5% and Lyla is at 2%."

"I'm losing to an idiot and someone who doesn't even want to run," Sophie said, exasperated.

"Just to be clear, I'm the one who doesn't want to run, right?" I asked.

17

S omething wasn't right. As I stood with Sophie, Sammie, Ben, and Luke in the Atrium a few minutes before Advisory was set to begin, I could tell something was brewing. There were a lot of stares in our direction, which disappeared quickly as soon as they were returned. There was giggling and even a few points.

I was at my breaking point when Tyler Nelson walked by and quipped, "Nice campaign video," and then continued on through the Atrium, chuckling to himself.

"What the heck is going on?" I asked.

Cheryl arrived simultaneously and said, "We have a problem."

"We just figured that out," Sophie said, "But we don't know what it is."

"Something about a campaign video?" Ben said.

"I can tell you, but it's probably best if I just show you." Cheryl slipped her phone out of her purse. She pulled up a text message and clicked on a video. "Someone from The Gazette sent this to me. It made the rounds last night on social media."

"What is it?" I asked.

"It's a fake campaign video. Jasmine Jane pretends to be Sophie."

Cheryl hit play and the video began. The intro screen said, 'Sophie Rodriguez- the anti-fun candidate.'

"Well, now we know Randy's behind this," Ben said.

The video continued. It cut to Jasmine Jane, a member of the Pretty Posse, wearing a curly wig, an exaggerated version of Sophie's hairstyle.

Jasmine, her body stiff and her voice monotone, said, "My name is Sophie Rodriguez. I'm the anti-fun candidate. But I mean that in a good way. I'm all about vegetables, and homework, and hosing kids off as they walk into school so they don't smell. If that sounds and smells good to you, vote for Sophie Rodriguez because a vote for Sophie means a vote for misery. Smell ya later! Or hopefully not!"

"I can't believe they would do that," Luke said.

I smirked at him.

"Okay, I can."

Sophie was biting her lower lip, trying to keep it together.

"Are you okay?" I asked, rubbing her shoulder.

She nodded, but didn't answer. I was afraid she was going to cry again.

And then Just Charles joined us with even more good news.

"We have a problem," he said. "Have you guys heard?"

"Of the fake campaign video?" Cheryl asked.

"No. All of Lyla's friends are telling everyone that Sophie has a boyfriend in Bear Creek." Bear Creek is the town next to ours.

That was the tipping point. Sophie rushed out of the Atrium, tears streaming down her face.

Lunch didn't get any better. Sophie, Ben, and Sammie were there. Cheryl was supposed to be heading our way with new polling data, but I hoped she wouldn't have any. Sophie wasn't handling things well.

Not only was she competitive and hated losing, but the Pretty Posse continued to needle her and the video that made fun of her really hurt her feelings. I had been on the receiving end of both issues in the past, so I knew how she felt.

My crew waited behind me on the hot lunch line. Miss Geller, the head lunch lady, and a generally nice woman, looked at me and said stiffly, "What can I get you?"

I scanned the options and said to myself, "What looks good?"

Miss Geller looked at Sophie and said, "Apparently, nothing."

"Chicken parm for me, please," I said.

"Same for me, Miss Geller," Sophie said.

Miss Geller ignored Sophie and slapped a piece of chicken parm on her plate. It was so hard, I thought it might shatter the plastic tray into a thousand pieces.

We pushed our trays down the line, waiting to pay.

Sophie whispered, "Why is she so mad?"

I whispered back, "You're telling everyone the food stinks."

"It does," she said, defensively.

I shrugged.

A voice called out from the back of the line. It was Jasmine Jane saying, "Oh, look, it's the carrot candidate."

I turned around and yelled, "They're good for your eyesight!" It was the best I could do.

Sophie just stared at her food as we made our way down the line. Eventually, we paid and grabbed our usual seats.

Sophie was shaken. As we got back to the table, I could see she was distracted.

"You can't let it get to you," I said.

"It already has. Why do they have to be so mean? Why can't they just focus on what they're gonna do and leave everyone else alone? They're trashing me on video, spreading rumors about fake boyfriends."

"I don't know," I said. I'm helpful like that.

Once we sat down, we all ate in silence until Ben said, "Why did I choose the French onion soup? It smells like fart onion soup."

"Mine looks like chicken phlegmigian," I said, poking the chicken with my spork.

"I hope they have the snotsbury steak tomorrow," Sammie said, laughing. "And what's with the twice-baked potato? Didn't they cook it long enough the first time?"

Sophie cracked a smile, but wasn't laughing like the rest of us were. Thankfully, she joined in and said, "At least the bratwurst is appropriately named."

We all laughed harder until Cheryl entered. She walked over to us with a bunch of papers in her hand.

I tried to send a message to keep the polling data to herself. I thought my bulging eyes and the shaking of my head would be an easy signal, but apparently, it was not.

Cheryl slipped into the seat next to Sammie and looked at Sophie. "I have bad news. The debates plus the video plus rumors that you're cheating on Austin has you sliding in the polls."

"How bad?" Sophie asked, her smile disappearing.

"You dropped another five points. Austin and Randy each picked up two and Lyla nabbed one."

"I'm getting sympathy votes now?" I asked. "This is terrible."

Sophie looked at me and said, "You know it's not true, right?"

"Of course," I said.

"I mean, why would I date someone in Bear Creek? They don't even have a Starbucks," Sophie deadpanned.

"Right, because that's all that matters in a relationship," Ben said.

"That's the only reason I date Ben," Sammie said. "He takes me to Scoops." She was referring to our favorite ice cream shop in town.

"I guess I've seen worse," I said, "Zorch and Miss Geller's relationship was built on meatloaf. The worst meatloaf ever."

"Which brings me back to our campaign. How are we gonna get better food here?" Sophie asked.

I was glad that she was focused on what we could do and not on what people were saying about her or on who they were voting for.

"You should probably lodge a complaint, to start," Sammie said.

"Can I ask a question?" I asked.

"Sure," Sophie said.

"If Bear Creek had a Starbucks, would you have a boyfriend there?"

Sophie cracked a smile. "Not unless you were there."

"Aww, I might puke into my food," Ben said. "And I wouldn't know the difference."

I looked at Sophie and said, "We gotta get you back."

"Yeah, we gotta find the Sophie that crushed the medieval quest," Sammie said.

"I think I have an idea," I said. "You ever been in a boys' bathroom?"

"Umm, what does that have to do with anything? I guess I have when I was a little kid with my dad."

"Well, we're gonna have to make a visit," I said.

Sophie looked at me like I was crazy. "Huh? Why would I want to go to the boys' bathroom?"

"We need to toughen you up," I said.

"How? The smell?"

"No, Max Mulvihill."

"You should go," Ben said. "I highly recommend it."

"This is so weird, guys," Sophie said. "But I have no reason not to trust you." She looked at Sammie and asked uncertainly, "Right?"

THE NEXT MORNING, Sophie met me outside of the high school. We had ten minutes before my science class started. I wasn't too concerned about me being late. I was more concerned that Sophie would get caught in between classes without having an I.D. And Principal Buthaire would know her.

The crowd was reasonably thick, as we headed down the west wing to Max's new space.

As we got closer, Sophie asked, "Are you sure I should be going in there?"

"It's under construction. There won't be anybody doing any personal business in there."

"Okay. If you say so."

I was wrong. Not about the personal business, but about going in there. I pushed open the door and allowed Sophie to pass. I took a few steps into the bathroom and was about to let go of the door when I heard the familiar and unwelcoming voice of Principal Butt Hair. I looked back at his smiling face.

Principal Buthaire said, "Oh, how lovely."

18

S ophie and I sat across from Principal Buthaire in his office. We called his former office back at Cherry Avenue Middle School, The Butt Crack. As he stared at us with a mischievous smile on his face, I thought about what to name his new office. Was it too boring to call it The Butt Crack? Should it be The Butt Crack #2 or 2.0? Or The Butt Bungalow? I decided not to decide just yet. A white-boarding, brain-storming session was the way to go to ensure the perfect name.

Finally, Principal Butt Hair spoke, "I wasn't sure how the day would turn out, but it's off to a marvelous start." He looked at Sophie and continued, "Miss Rodriguez, I see you didn't take my advice about watching who you spent your time with. And I also see that you were trespassing. You are not a student of this high school. I can only assume you are up to no good."

Sophie hated Principal Buthaire almost as much as I did. She looked at me and said, "Yes, I solemnly swear."

I tried not to laugh. If only we had Harry Potter's Marauder's Map, we would've avoided the situation entirely.

Principal Buthaire didn't appear to pick up on the H.P. reference, which was not surprising.

"This is no joking matter. Trespassing is a serious offense."

"Yes, sir. I know," Sophie said.

"What are you doing here and why were you going into an unauthorized area? Were you going to smoochie smoochie this early in the morning?"

I was thankful that he wasn't asking me any of those questions. We hadn't planned for the worst-case scenario of getting caught by Prince Butt Hair and didn't have a ready-made response.

Sophie thought for a moment and said, "Yes, we were going to smoochie smoochie. With Austin being in high school now, we don't see each other enough."

My face went red. It wasn't even true, but it still embarrassed me.

"That's all I need to know," Principal Buthaire said, holding up his hand. It seemed to make him more uncomfortable than both Sophie and me.

"Should we involve the police?" Principal Buthaire pondered aloud.

"Please, sir," Sophie said. "It won't happen again."

"I'm feeling generous. With those duct tape wackos wreaking havoc around here, it feels good to get a win. No need to go crazy and involve the authorities. This time," he said, firmly.

"Thank you," Sophie and I said, together.

"Austin, you get a week's detention for being out of bounds. Sophie, the same, plus another two weeks for the trespassing, assuming Ms. Pierre agrees to that. I will call her immediately."

"She calls it after-school character enhancement now, just so you two are on the same page," I said.

"Ooh, I like the sound of that. Can I steal that?" Principal Buthaire asked.

I shrugged. "Sure?"

"This truly is a marvelous day. Now, be on your way. Oh, and Misterrrr Davenport, you're late for first period." He tore off a detention slip and handed it to me. "Add this to the others. Now, scram."

Sophie and I booked out of there. You never wanted to linger around the principal's office, particularly a principal like Butt Hair.

I walked Sophie to the exit. "I'll see you over there at lunch."

Sophie nodded, her face anxious. "We have to keep this quiet. Oh, and great idea," she said, sarcastically.

"Sorry."

I hustled to science. It was pretty uneventful. My trip between schools was a lot more eventful. Like off the charts.

I like to get a head start between science and advisory so I can beat the crowd and spend some time with my friends before middle school starts. My books were packed up before the bell rang. Thankfully, it hadn't been changed to a whistle just yet, although I heard that Mr. Muscalini was behind a district-wide push to do just that.

As soon as the bell rang, I grabbed my bag and rushed out of the classroom. I hit the hallway with some speed, and it was with perfect timing. I had nothing but open road ahead of me. I revved up the sports car that was my nerdy, adolescent body and speed-walked down the hall. I think the revving might've been a bit too loud as I failed to hear the commotion approaching me from behind.

I felt the wind at my back. I was moving so fast; I couldn't believe it. I thought I might be flying. I looked down at the floor and I was! My feet were moving, but I was literally six inches off the ground! I looked around in shock.

To my left, I saw a dude with a pole attached to some duct tape and the same thing to my right. My heart sank, as did the rest of me, right into the hard floor, face first. I slid for a second and then came to an abrupt stop, the duct tape taking hold on the floor. Pain surged from my knees to my cheeks- my upper cheeks. My lower cheeks were fine until someone stepped on them, as he or she walked across my body that was taped to the floor.

I struggled to get up, but there was too much tape and I had missed a bunch of upper body workouts. Like, all of them.

"How does the floor taste, nerd?" Someone yelled as they passed by, laughing.

"It could use some salt. And less dirt," I said. "But it's still better than the cafeteria."

After a few minutes, the hallways emptied out enough that kids stopped walking across me. They had enough room to ignore my decrepit body as they passed by, which was at least somewhat appreciated. True, it would've been nice if someone had actually helped me up, but not stepping on me was also helpful in a way.

I lay there for a minute after the bell rang, not sure what

to do. Struggling didn't seem to work all that well. I tried to gnaw at the duct tape around my shoulder, but couldn't fully reach. My head was pounding, probably from all of the stepping on my head that occurred, and struggling made it worse, so I just lay there, helpless. Thankfully, Cheeks turned the corner pushing a cloud of dust with his broom.

Cheeks thrust the broom a little too closely to me. Dust filled my lungs. I really could've done without more organ damage, but there was nothing I could do. Cheeks was no Zorch.

I looked up at him feebly and whispered, "Help me."

Cheeks didn't say anything. He just squatted down in front of me and pushed the butt of his broom toward my face. My eyes widened, but he didn't poke me with it. I guess I was conditioned to expect harm at that point. He slipped the broom handle under the duct tape next to my shoulder, slipping it down my arm. He used the broom as a lever. With a grunt, the duct tape tore from the floor with a rip.

Once I got to my feet, regained my senses, and dusted myself off, I thanked Cheeks and was about to head over the Cherry Avenue Middle when Principal Buthaire appeared before me.

"In the halls after the bell. That's a detention."

"But I don't have any more classes here. I'm going back to Cherry Avenue."

Principal Buthaire just shook his head and stared at me for a moment. I didn't know what to do.

Finally, he spoke, "You're only in high school one period a day and you're wreaking more havoc than you did in a full day in middle school."

"And I'm not even trying. I'm a natural, I guess."

Principal Butt Hair looked like his head might explode. His face was a shade of purple that I had never seen before.

"I'm sorry, sir. I thought you were giving me a compliment."

"No, it wasn't a compliment! I have been trying to catch these duct tape bandits since I took over last year! You're finally going to help me maintain some order around here! Let's go to my office!"

I waited for an hour outside of The Bureau of Butt Hair. What do you think of that one? I'm not married to it. Anyway, a police sketch artist finally arrived. I described the perpetrators, but for some reason, Principal Buthaire wasn't happy.

When the sketch artist showed him the drawing, he grabbed it and tore it into pieces.

"What the heck is this? It's just some kid's butt in jeans!"

"That's all I saw! I was taped to the floor."

"Get out of my sight!"

Gladly. I got up and walked out. I could still make it to lunch. Oh, joy. I could almost taste the buttermilk barfcakes.

19

I finally made it back to middle school. Buttermilk barfcakes were the least of my concern. I rushed into lunch to meet up with my crew. Sophie's campaign was in serious crisis mode. I could see on their faces that something was wrong.

I went straight over to our table without even grabbing lunch. I wasn't hungry. It was probably nausea brought on by the concussion I most likely received in the high school student stampede.

I slipped into my usual seat next to Sophie as they were talking animatedly about a scandal.

Cheryl's mouth was motoring like Evil Chuck in a candy store.

"Whoa! Can you slow down or catch me up to speed?" I said.

"We're having a campaign crisis," Cheryl said, angrily. "Your bathroom idea is tanking Sophie's campaign."

"What do you mean?" I asked.

"Somehow, Randy found out and is spreading rumors that I got arrested and I can't be trusted," Sophie said.

It was unreal how quickly Randy's campaign reacted. By the end of the day, they had a poster of Sophie up in the atrium. It had a picture of Sophie's face on an old picture of me in my prison costume from when I took a stand against Butt Hair's prison rules. Across the top, it read, 'Do you really want a criminal as your President?' and beneath it, 'Vote for Randy Warblemacher- the integrity candidate.'

Sophie looked at the poster and said, "I can't believe this."

"I know I need to work out," I said.

"Really?" Sophie asked, annoyed.

"This is wrong," I said. I grabbed the poster from both sides and tore it down.

I looked at Sophie and said, "We're gonna bounce back. We have to catch Randy in a lie. On tape- proving how corrupt he is."

"He's too ruthless and good at cheating."

"He's one of the best," I said. "But maybe we can bug his campaign headquarters?"

"What're you gonna do? Break into his house?" Sophie asked.

"Does he have a doggie door?" I asked.

"Funny," Sophie said. I had gotten stuck in her doggie door a while back. It wasn't my best moment. The whole town was upset that we ran out of butter for a week. "Do you think Randy has a dog?"

"No, you're right. He's a snake person. He's the Voldemort of middle school." And then I had an idea. "Let's bash me with posters. We can drive my numbers to zero. You should be able to crush Randy then."

"Aww, you would do that for me?"

"Of course. I just need the picture back of me swinging on the harness from Santukkah!"

"But that's my favorite picture of you," Sophie protested.

"It's just for a day. I need to turn it into a poster. Would you really want to vote for me in my Batman underwear?"

"You're totally gonna tank. This is gonna be awesome."

"Thanks, but you're a little too excited."

"Sorry," Sophie said, sheepishly.

"There's Randy. Here we go," I said.

"What are you gonna do?" Sophie asked.

"I'm gonna catch him in a lie. We're gonna take down his campaign." I pressed record on my voice recorder app on my phone and slipped it into my pocket.

"Good luck," Sophie said.

I walked over to Randy. He was talking with Nick in a bigger group that also had Regan and the Pretty Posse.

Randy saw me as I stepped toward him. "Well, well, well. It's Austin Davenfart. How does it feel to be on the verge of losing the election?"

"I don't care about the election. I've made that pretty clear. But you already know that since you were the one who got me all the signatures and entered me into the election."

Randy smiled. For a moment, I didn't think he was going to say anything about it. And then he went and ruined his campaign. Randy leaned in and said, "That was a particularly good idea of mine. I Goblet of Fired you. Sophie by herself might've been tough to beat, but with you in the contest, I get the best of both worlds- Sophie can't win and I get to beat you."

If I hadn't just caught him in a huge lie, I probably would've gotten sick. For two reasons. First, he's just so disgustingly devious. And two, the idea that he read Harry Potter was somehow very disheartening. I'm sure he rooted for Malfoy and Voldemort, but still, it took me a while to get over it.

"Why are you so excited?" Randy asked.

"No reason," I said, smirking. It felt good to smirk at him for once. I had him right where I wanted him. He was on tape confessing to rigging the election. "You're going down, Warblecheater. Down to Chinatown."

"In your dreams."

"You think I dream about you going to Chinatown?"

"Yeah, that is kind of a stretch, even for you, Dork wad."

"Enjoy your moment in the spotlight. A dark cloud is coming your way."

20

I walked back to Sophie and crew, all smiles.

Sophie said, "What happened? That was pretty quick."

"I got something. We got him right where we want him to be. If he doesn't resign in shame, he's going to get bounced from the election for fraud. Let's go see Dr. Dinkledorf."

I grabbed Sophie's hand and pulled her through the hallway.

"What could he possibly have told you in thirty seconds?"

"Thirty seconds is a long time. We talked the election, his cheating ways. We talked about Harry Potter, his dreams, Chinatown. It was a nice conversation."

"How is that possible?"

"I'm that good," I said.

"We'll see about that," Sophie said, as we rushed into Dr. Dinkledorf's classroom.

He looked up from a stack of papers that he was grading. "Hello, there! To what do I owe the pleasure?"

I dragged Sophie over to Dr. Dinkledorf's desk. "Randy admitted to cheating in the election and I've got it all on tape."

"Those are serious accusations, but let's hear what you've got."

I pulled out my phone and pressed play on the recording. It started with muffled voices. Both Dr. Dinkledorf and Sophie looked at me, confused.

I said, "Don't worry. That was probably just during my walk over. It's coming."

Oh, boy, was it coming. It was quiet for a split second then a fart reverberated through the speakers. They both looked at me disgusted.

"It wasn't me!" I thought it was silent. I guessed that since the phone was in my pocket it was much easier to pick up my butt talking than my mouth. And Randy's mouth was gonna be even harder to capture.

The recording continued for another minute, muffled voices rumbling the entire time. The recording ended. I feared that Sophie would end me.

"A compelling argument, I must say, Austin," Dr. Dinkledorf said, scratching his head.

"I don't know what happened. It was clear as day. He told me that he signed me up because he wanted to split the vote between me and Sophie, so he could win and get enjoyment out of beating me."

"I'm sorry. But there's nothing I can do. Without proof, it's just your word against his. And while I trust you completely, there is no way that this will hold up if it goes to Ms. Pierre or the Board of Education."

I looked and Sophie and said, "I'm sorry. I really messed this up."

Sophie looked like she might cry. I didn't know what to

do to help her. I kept trying to, but it either didn't ever work or worse, it backfired.

"Keep fighting the good fight, Sophie," Dr. Dinkledorf said. "You're running a strong campaign. You're the only candidate with a real message."

I WAS in the dumps for the rest of the day and night. I worked on a bunch of poster ideas with Cheryl to trash my campaign. Her father, Mr. Van Snoogle-Something, ran a print shop. He had helped me out with posters before, when Sophie and I were trying to win Cupid's Cutest Couple Contest. Even though we had some great ideas, I was pretty bummed. And the next morning wasn't much better. Unless, of course, you thought I had started to enjoy the soothing nature of being duct taped to various surfaces

The next morning, I exited the bus outside of the high school. I was still half asleep. I zombie-walked to the side of the bus, waiting for Barney to get off so we could head to class together. It was a bad decision.

With the stealth of ninjas, two kids from the duct tape troop strapped me to the side of the bus with a wall of tape. I was so tired; I didn't even try to fight against it. They laughed as they ran off.

Barney got off the bus and did a double take when he saw me. Leighton did the same, but added an older-sister eye roll.

"We'll get you out of here," Barney said, picking at the corner of the tape.

"Just leave me, man," I said, defeated.

"I hear you. I'm starting to enjoy them, too. It's kind of therapeutic, like my weighted blanket."

Leighton joined in. "There's one problem. You're strapped to the side of the bus. I'd probably get in trouble with mom and dad if I left you."

"Thanks for your concern for my well-being."

"Do they put extra glue on these?" Leighton asked. "I can't get it off."

"I don't know. Cheeks had to use his broom as a lever to get me out last time," I said.

Some kids laughed as they got off the bus. Other kids stared. And still more acted like it was just another day with a kid taped to the side of a giant, yellow school bus.

Leighton put her hands behind my shoulders and pulled. Nothing happened.

"This isn't good," she said.

Barney started pulling my feet. I could barely see what was going on down there, but there was a whole lot of grunting and groaning. And then the Barn Door flew open as my shoes slipped off my feet, the momentum of Barney's efforts causing him to tumble back onto the sidewalk. He banged into the legs of the hulking Flea.

"Whoa, bro! What are you doing down there?"

The bus doors shut and its engine revved. I quickly changed my mind about wanting to stick around on the side of the bus. Don't get me wrong, there were some potential benefits to it. I would've gotten to take the bus to school with Ben and Sammie again. True, I'd be on the outside, but still, I wasn't willing to risk my life for that. Call me crazy.

"Oh, my God! Nobody told the bus driver!" Leighton yelled, and then didn't actually attempt to tell the bus driver.

"The bus is taking off! Flea, I need your help!" I yelled.

Flea looked over at me and his eyes bulged. "I'm coming, little buddy!"

Flea knocked over two kids as he exploded toward me

like a football lineman about to crush the quarterback. Yeah, they probably had a few broken bones, but it was a small price to pay for my safety.

The bus started beeping and backing up out of its parking space.

"Hurry!" Leighton yelled.

Flea reached down with his boulder-sized hands and wrapped them around my straw-like ankles. He pulled with a high-pitched scream. Or perhaps that was me as I hit Mach three speed. Flea pulled so hard I thought he might've torn a worm hole in the universe.

I landed on top of Flea who was flat on his back, my feet in his face. I looked up at the sky and felt the sun warming my body. And then I realized that nurturing warmth was hitting my bare skin. I looked over at the bus pulling away and saw my t-shirt dangling on the side of the bus, held on by a piece of torn duct tape.

"No! That's my favorite shirt!" I yelled.

I rolled off of Flea and we both made it to our feet.

Thankfully, there were only a few people around at that point, but all of them were trying not to laugh as I stood there in my jeans and sneakers, wondering why the universe did that to me.

I didn't really know what to say. I was pretty embarrassed. I decided on, "You guys want to see my armpit hair? I named him 'Hairy Pitter.'"

Leighton walked away, shaking her head.

"You okay, little buddy?" Flea asked. "You can have my shirt," he said.

"I appreciate that, but I've been embarrassed enough today. I'd rather not look like I was wearing a dress."

"That makes sense," he said.

"What am I supposed to do now?" I asked.

And then Barney came to the rescue. He reached into his backpack and pulled out a t-shirt. "Here, take this. It's my gym shirt."

"What are you gonna do? I don't want to take this."

"No, you're doing me the favor. Now, I have an excuse not to participate in gym. Mr. Flexen should give me a pass."

"Is gym in high school as bad as middle school?"

"It's worse."

"How could it be worse? I thought that was impossible."

"The kids are bigger and stronger. They throw stuff harder at you, but I'm just as much of a nerd as I was in middle school."

"Oh, dude. I'm not ready for that."

I put the t-shirt on and headed into school with Flea and the Barn Door.

"Thanks, guys. I appreciate the help."

"No problem," Flea said.

"Any time," Barney said. "Really. I'll give you my gym shirt every day."

As we headed into class, I tried to look on the bright side. I was alive and at least there wasn't any glue stuck to my clothes that time. True, part of the reason I was glue free was because my clothes were torn from my body, not to mention the force that vaporized the rest of it. But, like I said, I was trying to look on the bright side. And then it hit me. Glue. If one fights fire with fire, I needed to fight glue with glue. I had a plan.

"Dude," I said to Barney, "find out where the duct tape bandits go or hide out after they duct tape us."

"I've heard that Principal Buthaire has been trying to figure that out since last year. It's a tough ask. But I'll do my best."

Thankfully, I escaped my morning at the high school

without any additional run-ins with the duct tape demons and walked as fast as I could over to middle school. I thought about asking Flea to tear a worm hole open for me or just chuck me across the campus, but he had already done enough for me that morning.

When I got into the atrium, it was chaos. Not rip-your-shirt-from-your-back-or-you-die chaos, but close. Jace Thompson stood on a bench with his bull horn calling out campaign slogans for Randy. People were hanging posters left and right. Zack was busy talking to people and looking at them mysteriously, while Lyla was trying to right her ship after the Mucas Massacre. She was handing out tissues with writing that said, 'Lyla's snot your average candidate.' I liked that she was trying to own it, but I wasn't convinced it would work.

I needed to figure out exactly how to take my campaign down a few notches to compete with those clowns, while helping Sophie to reenergize her own. And it needed gigawatts of energy. I headed over to my crew. Everyone was gathered in a circle, looking at the latest polling data.

I hoped for better numbers for Sophie, but based on the looks on their faces, they weren't better.

Cheryl looked up at me. "Latest polls are in. You and Sophie are basically tied for second with 26% each. Randy is at 42%."

"That's better than last time," I said. I looked at Sophie and said, "You're gaining."

"Not enough," Sophie said.

"Now that everyone thinks that Sophie got arrested, her numbers are climbing. It's offset the anti-fun spin that Randy has been pushing."

"Can convicts be president?" Luke asked.

"I'm not really a convict, idiot," Sophie said.

"Oh, yeah. Forgot."

"When is my underwear poster arriving?" I asked Cheryl. "And I've got another idea for a poster and maybe even a video." I was thinking I might introduce everyone to Hairy Pitter. Who would vote for a kid who names his armpit hair? Nobody. Not even the clowns in Gopherville.

Cheryl said, "My dad should have it here this afternoon. This is all here for the taking. We can catch Randy. We just have to find a way for you to lose votes."

"I've been trying. I'm just too likeable," I said, flashing my best smile.

"You're not that likeable right now," Sophie said.

"Touché."

Cheryl continued, "Election Day is rapidly approaching. When I was covering the election last year for the Gopher Gazette, I noticed that the last week was the week everybody made a big push."

"You mean it gets crazier than last week?" Sophie asked.

"Pretty much."

MY BATMAN POSTER arrived at the end of the day. Cheryl and Mr. Van Snoogle-Something hung it up in the atrium. It was awesome, outside of the fact that I had to relive the embarrassment of swinging on stage in front of hundreds of people in my Batman underwear.

I wasn't sure how long it was going to stay up on the wall, though. Apparently, I started a trend. After tearing down Randy's rude poster of Sophie as the anti-fun candidate, everyone seemed to think it was fair game to start tearing down everyone else's posters.

They were getting torn down and replaced faster than

people could even see them. Our crew started putting cafeteria food leftovers around the edges and on the backs of our posters so if somebody did try to take one down, they would get radiation poisoning. Just kidding. I think.

New posters popped up like they were digital billboards or something. People who weren't even running were putting up signs. Someone put a 'Harry Potter 4 President' sign up. Our own idiot, Luke, put up a sign that read, 'Not running for anything. I just wanted a sign and some attention.'

And Randy seemed to have an unlimited budget. We surmised that he was being bankrolled by either his own parents or Regan's parents. He was churning out posters left and right. He had videos hitting social media twice a day. I'm pretty certain he had editors and a makeup artist on staff. I made a note to remind myself to make fun of Randy for wearing make up the next time he took a dig at me.

The swag was getting out of hand, too. I mentioned the tissues, which was witty, but not all that impactful. Once you blew your nose, it was done. T-shirts and buttons had a more lasting effect and were less disgusting.

The Pretty Posse was out in full swing, fake smiles and laughs, along with plenty of over-the-shoulder hair flips. They were giving out pins and t-shirts with Randy's stupid face on it.

I heard Regan say sweetly to Tina Brunson, "Vote for Randy," and then threateningly, "If you know what's good for you."

～

THE NEXT MORNING, Dr. Dinkledorf attempted to put a stop to all the craziness. As I sat in Advisory, the Speaker of

Doom crackled to life. Dr. D. said, "It has become apparent that the election campaigning is getting out of control. From now until Election Day, there will be no gizmos, gadgets, or thingamabobs allowed. Furthermore, each candidate is only allowed one poster in each common area: the Atrium, the cafeteria, and outside the library."

Just Charles leaned over to me and said, "One poster? That's crazy."

"Yeah, how are we gonna catch up?" I thought for a minute. And then I had an idea. "Can you work with Cheryl on putting all of Sophie's posters together into one giant one? We can get Zorch to help us hang it."

Just Charles smiled broadly. "Absolutely. We'll get a step up on Randy. And don't forget, your arm pit video went out this morning. It's gonna go viral."

And he was right. It went viral, but it had the opposite effect than we had planned. I thought that by naming my first armpit hair, Hairy Pitter, I would tank my campaign, but that would give the voting public of Cherry Avenue Middle School way too much credit.

But I didn't know it until I was heading to lunch and saw Miley Schwab. She tapped me on the shoulder as she caught up to me in the hallway.

"Austin, that was the funniest video I've ever seen."

"Thanks," I said, smiling. "I'm hoping people will realize I don't want to be president and that they shouldn't vote for me."

"Are you kidding? Everyone loved it. They think you're mocking the system. Have a great day!" Miley said, turning the corner toward the science wing.

I knew for certain that I would not be having a great day.

"What is wrong with these people?" I asked no one in particular.

I walked into the cafeteria and nearly bumped into Sophie and Cheryl, who were staring at the latest polling data. Sophie snatched the paper out of Cheryl's hand and hurled it at the wall. I thought the floor beneath me might've shook.

"Nice video, Hairy Pitter," Cheryl said, shaking her head.

21

I t only got worse from there. Well, I did avoid getting duct taped to the bus the next morning, but after that, it got worse. First, Barney told me he had no luck in finding out where the duct tapers go after they strike.

"Dude, they disappear. They have different perpetrators every time, route changes, technique changes. It's the perfect crime," Barney said, scratching his head.

I wasn't convinced that it was the perfect crime, but they were pretty good. I wanted to take them down worse than ever. My frustration in every other important area of my life, namely tanking the school election and being a good boyfriend, fueled my motivation for revenge against the duct tape dorks.

But very quickly, I developed bigger issues. We had a science lab, our most complicated of the year to that point. Flea was really into science, ever since I explained the science around burping and farting. He insisted on leading our two-man team in the lab. I wasn't gonna argue with him. Plus, I was still grateful that he saved my life.

It proved to be one of the worst mistakes I've ever made.

It started innocently enough. Flea squeezed the container he was attempting to open and nearly obliterated it. Baking soda flew everywhere, including my face. My goggles were coated with so much powder that I couldn't see anything. I took off my goggles and leaned over the lab table toward the sink.

As I rinsed the goggles off, I glanced over at what Flea was doing. I thought he was cleaning up the baking soda, but he ended up mixing it with something that had explosive potential. Even more explosive than the flatulent fondue from the cafeteria.

I yelled, "No!" But it was too late.

Sparks expanded into an explosion as the compounds combined. I turned away, but even with my cat-like reflexes, I was too slow. We were both hit by a puff of fire. The warmth hit my face with force. It took me a minute to regroup as I could feel my face flushed with redness. And it wasn't embarrassment this time. It was burning red.

Miss Kelvin rushed over. I stood up when she arrived.

"Is everybody okay? What happened?" she asked.

"I think so," Flea said.

I didn't respond.

Flea looked at me and said, "You really should use some sunscreen, bro. And get some eyebrows."

"Huh?" I touched my face. It felt okay. And then my heart dropped. I felt my face again and nearly puked. My eyebrows were missing!

"Where are my eyebrows?" I screamed.

Everyone started searching frantically for my eyebrows, as if finding them would somehow fix the fact that they had been blown off my face.

Brie Kuster yelled out excitedly, "They're over here!"

I rushed over to Brie. My eyes followed her pointing

finger. My eyebrows were attached to a picture of a scientist holding a beaker with a sign that read, 'Science is a blast!'

"This is fascinating," Miss Kelvin said, leaning in to study them. "The heat from the explosion caused your eyebrows to melt into the plastic of the poster."

"Yeah, really fascinating," I said. "What am I supposed to do without eyebrows?"

Flea said, "Here let me draw some on you." He grabbed the back of my head with one hand while holding a marker in the other.

Miss Kelvin and I both yelled, "No!"

But it was too late. Again. Flea stuck his tongue out as he concentrated. I was afraid I might drown in the saliva. He ran the marker over each eye where my beautiful eyebrows used to be.

"Oh, God," I said, as Flea let go with a smile.

"Not bad," he said.

"Yeah?" I asked, unsure.

Brie and Miss Kelvin were surer than I was.

Brie said, "You look. Well, you look."

I think Miss Kelvin was speechless.

I didn't like the sound of that. Not Miss Kelvin's speech-lessness, but Brie's comment. I pushed through the crowd around me and found my way to a mirror over the sink.

"It's a real-life brow beating," I whimpered.

Flea looked at the scientist wearing my eyebrows. "I never noticed he was so mad," he said, scratching his head.

"Those aren't his eyebrows. They're mine," I said, angrily.

"Right," Flea said, turning to me. "Why are you so mad?"

"You blew my eyebrows off. And then drew on whatever these things are," I said, annoyed.

"Oh, yeah. Right."

I looked in the mirror again. My new eyebrows were too high and too arched. I looked like I was in a perpetual state of shock, which I might actually have been, so perhaps it was fitting for the moment, but eventually I would not be shocked. Then what?

I whispered, "My brows. My beautiful brows."

I walked over to the lab table and turned on the sink. I grabbed some paper towels and loaded them up with soap. After I got a good lather going on the paper towel, I scrubbed my eyebrows like I'd never scrubbed anything in my entire life. My whole class was waiting to see what would happen.

I lowered the paper towel and saw that there was some black on it. I was cautiously optimistic, until I heard the groans.

"They were one of my best features," I whimpered.

"Let's have a moment of science for Austin's eyebrows," Brie said.

Miss Kelvin broke out into a laughing snort. It was really encouraging.

I shook my head and headed to the bathroom. I needed to talk to Max about the duct taping. And while I was at it, I hoped he knew someone involved in eyebrow reconstruction.

I pushed the door open to Max's and walked into the bathroom.

"Whoa! Who the heck are you? Oh, Austin. Dude. What happened to you?"

"Science," was all I could say. "You know anybody who can fix this?"

"That's above my pay grade, man. I'm sorry. Anything else I can help with?"

"Yeah, I need to figure out how to stop getting duct taped to things around the school. I need to set a trap for them. Any idea where they hide out?"

"That I can help with. They sometimes use the storage room down on the west wing."

"How do you know this stuff?"

"Dude, we've known each other for more than two years. It's my job to know. How's the election going?"

"Not great. I was trying to get Sophie in here to see you. She needs a confidence boost, but we got snared by Butt Hair."

"That sounds lovely."

"It was not," I said, shaking my head.

"I can help her, but I'm not planning on leaving this bathroom until 2040."

"Really?" I asked, surprised.

"Well, no. Not literally. It just has to look like it's 2040, but that's gonna take a week or so."

"I can't risk breaking her in here again. Buthaire will throw her into jail."

"It's gonna have to wait then."

"It can't."

"Sorry, bro. I'm hemorrhaging cash here. I need to start generating some revenue."

"I understand. Thanks, anyway."

To make matters worse, I was late leaving the school. Guess who just happened to be patrolling the hallway, looking for delinquents? You got that right, Principal Buthaire.

"In the hallway after the bell again, Misterrrr Davenport," Prince Butt Hair sighed. "This is getting anti-climactic." He looked at me quizzically. "How is it possible that you're surprised? I give you detention all the time."

"I'm not surprised," I said.

"Your eyebrows tell a different story."

"I'm aware of that, sir. They got blown off in science. You'll be hearing from my lawyer." I didn't really have a lawyer, unless you counted the clown that showed up at my hearing last year when I was going to be expelled. But he didn't have to know that.

"Oh, did I say detention? We can let you slide on that one. I mean, I think we've been growing closer these past few years, haven't we?"

"Oh, definitely, sir," I lied. "Have a fantastic day."

"You as well, Austin."

Somehow, I was able to exit the high school without cracking up. I may have lost my eyebrows, but I found a way to untangle myself from the stranglehold of Butt Hair.

22

I walked over to the middle school, my eyebrows, or at least the region that used to contain my eyebrows, was starting to burn. I feared the rest of my face would burn red in embarrassment when I walked into the Atrium with my magic marker eyebrows that were anything but magic.

A sixth grader held the door for me as I approached the school. I think he did it out of fear. Most of the other kids just scattered when they saw me. As I entered the Atrium, I held my hand across my naked forehead, pretending to be stressed or perhaps shading the sun as I looked out into the distance. I could handle the typical insult, but not even the most confident person in the world could endure the predicament I was in.

I walked over to Sophie, Ben, Sammie, Cheryl, and Just Charles.

"Whatever you do," I whispered, "don't make a big deal."

"Holy farts!" Just Charles yelled at the top of his lungs, staring at my less-than artistic eyebrows.

The entire school looked in my direction.

"Thanks for that," I said, grumpily.

"Oh. My. God." Randy cackled from a few groups over, staring in my direction. "This is the best day of my life." Randy, Regan, Nick, and Jasmine all cracked up.

I didn't even bother to respond.

"Your life must be pretty sad if someone's eyebrows make your life," Ben said, angrily.

"You're lucky you're not wearing a bathing suit," Regan said to Ben, smirking, referring to the time she pushed Ben into the pool.

Ben gulped, and turned his back to them.

"Don't listen to them," Sophie said.

"I kind of remember telling you the same thing," I said.

"Touché," Sophie said, smirking.

"What. The. Heck. Happened?" Sammie asked, her eyes bulging.

"Flea made a mistake during our science lab and blew off my eyebrows. And then tried to fix it by drawing new ones. So, a typical day in my life."

"Smile, Davenfart!" Randy yelled, excitedly while snapping a picture of me on his phone.

I was certain nothing bad would come of that.

ON MY WAY TO ADVISORY, I bumped into Dr. Dinkledorf. He was so old, I was pretty certain he didn't even notice my eyebrows.

"Austin, my boy. We have a bit of a problem. Do you mind telling Sophie that her oversized poster is technically within the rules, but a violation of the spirit of the rules? She's going to have to take it down. But we're going to change the poster rules. Each candidate will now have four posters, one on each wall of the atrium, and one each by the cafeteria, er five-star whatever, and outside the library, and cannot be changed for the remainder of the election. Did she change the name of the library?"

"Don't know. Okay, sir," I said. "We'll take care of it. "See you later."

I turned around to see Mr. Muscalini walking toward me, admiring his biceps. I was surprised he even noticed me. He frowned and asked, "You shave your eyebrows, Davenport?"

"No, sir. Just a science accident. Flea did it."

"Great football player. Not the sharpest tool in the shed, though. I shave my back sometimes. Don't worry. It grows back."

"Thanks for that. It's really helpful."

MY MOTHER WAS able to remove most of the magic marker with rubbing alcohol, but not the whole thing. I still looked like a weirdo, but I didn't look so surprised anymore. I leaned more toward expressionless.

It was painful walking into science class the next day, seeing my eyebrows on another person. If you've never been through that, I don't wish it on anyone. Well, maybe Randy. I tried to think about ways to reattach them, but glue was the only thing I could think of and I wasn't too keen on that idea. Plus, I still hadn't figured out how to extract my eyebrows from the melted plastic.

When I got to middle school, one of the first people I saw was Zack. He was handing out fake mustaches to everyone. I know Dr. Dinkledorf said no more gadgets and gizmos, but nobody really knew what he was talking about.

"Davenport, you want a mustache?" Zack asked.

"Why are you handing out mustaches?"

"I'm the mysterious mustache candidate," Zack scoffed.

"You don't even have a mustache."

"I do, too!"

"It looks like you just drank chocolate milk."

Zack's face dropped. I mean, his face didn't fall off or anything. After my eyebrow incident, I felt the need to clarify.

"Please don't tell anyone! It could ruin my campaign."

I laughed. "I think you've done that already, by basing it all on having a non-existent mustache." I looked down at the mustaches in his box. "Give me two mustaches and your secret is safe with me."

"Done."

I took two of them, peeled the stickers off the back, and put them on in place of eyebrows. They were a little bushy, but I didn't like being bald in the eyebrow region. I felt like my whole face was naked.

Then I saw a new poster and stopped dead in my tracks. It was a picture of me without my eyebrows! And is read, 'All nerds matter!' I slumped over as I walked to my crew.

"What's wrong?" Ben asked.

"Randy's putting more thought into my campaign than Zack is into his own. We're never gonna win."

"Excuse me, everyone," Randy's voice boomed through Jace's bull horn. "I would like to invite everyone, even you average- and below-average kids, to my election victory party. It will be held at a special venue with a performance by Love Puddle! Details to follow!"

The crowd cheered. Even Luke was clapping. I stared him down. "Oh, sorry," he said. "Just got caught up in the moment."

Sophie and I looked at each other.

"We need a strategy session," she said.

"Give up?" I asked.

She glared at me.

23

We held our strategy session at lunch. It was Rump Roast Day. Don't ask. I sat next to Sophie, as usual, with Ben, Cheryl, and Just Charles.

"I don't know what to do anymore." Sophie said. "I should just make up stuff like Randy."

"You don't need to make promises you can't keep," Cheryl said. "People like that you stand for something."

"Not everyone."

"I agree with Cheryl," I said. "But you need to spice things up, Soph. You can't be all salad bars and art programs."

"What's a fart program?" Ben asked.

Cheryl shook her head. "Oh, God. I think you should get your hearing checked." She looked at me and said, "And then we have the Austin issue."

"I'm an issue now? I don't know what to say. My stupidity is not costing me votes."

"Your stupidity is remarkably charming," Sophie said.

"I guess I should be thankful for that. It's the reason I have Sophie."

"That's true," Ben said.

"It's okay. I own it. I can't drop out of the election. And I'm just too dang likable."

"Yeah, and nobody likes me," Sophie said, tears welling up in her eyes. "I just can't believe how everyone's treated me and how unfair they've all been." She wiped her tears away. "Why do I care so much about what all these idiots think? I even care what Regan thinks about me."

I put my arm around Sophie. "I'm gonna try to talk to Max again."

Ben looked at me, tentatively.

"Do you all know who Max Mulvihill is?"

Cheryl said, "I've been investigating him for the past two years. I'm gonna break a huge story about him and the misuse of public school bathrooms."

"Well, he moved out of the middle school, so I'm sorry to say, that story is dead. And he's a good dude. He's helped me out of more than a few jams."

Just Charles said, "Oh, thank God. I thought I was crazy. Who has bathrooms like that in public school or anywhere?"

I said, "Max was the reason we won Battle of the Bands."

"He cured my stage fright," Ben said.

"He saved my cousin from getting deported," Just Charles said.

"I want to meet him," Sophie said. "But not in the boys' bathroom. Burger Boys?"

"I'll see what I can do."

24

The campaigning continued pretty much as it had. Sophie continued to get bashed by Randy while our squad had no answers on how to respond. Or at least nothing that worked. There was a fake poster of Sophie saying that she wanted more tests and to ban buses so that kids could walk to school to get more exercise. It was not well received.

I wondered if I should just ask Flea and his crew to duct tape Randy to the wall or something. His credibility as the cool kid would take an instant hit. But I didn't wish that on anyone. My focus shifted to the duct tape terrors. I remembered my earlier thought about fighting glue with glue.

When I got home from school, I headed into the garage. I knew my dad had tons of leftover stuff from all of the projects he worked on. There had to be glue somewhere. I scanned the shelves and quickly found a nearly-full container of wood floor glue.

"Noyce," I said out loud. "But how will I spread this?" I looked around and said, "Paint rolla...."

I grabbed the glue and a paint roller. Now, all I had to do

was set the trap without getting caught myself. But how? I headed inside and put the duct-tape defeating materials in my school bag. I would have to have Ben take my books to school for me.

I thought for a moment on how to get to the storage facility, lay out the glue, and get out of there without being caught while also being on time for science. I would have to get there early.

Miss Kelvin was the answer. I took out my phone and opened the app we used to communicate with our teachers. I texted, 'Can I come in early tomorrow? I want to make sure I have everything set for the test. I've missed quality study time mourning the loss of my eyebrows.'

She wrote back quickly, 'Sure! Should we have a funeral for your brows for closure?'

'I'll be okay,' I wrote. '7:30?'

'See you then. A moment of science...I'm still cracking up about that!'

I'm glad she found it all so amusing.

THE NEXT MORNING, I awoke with a new hope. I didn't know how Sophie was going to win the election, but I was optimistic duct tape would no longer play such a debilitating role in my life.

My mother dropped me off at school at about 7:15. I walked past the security guard, my backpack bulging with home improvement supplies.

"Good morning," I said to the burly guard. "Meeting Miss Kelvin for extra help."

The guard nodded without a word. I had ten minutes to lay my glue trap. I walked quickly through the halls, hoping to avoid anyone and everyone, and especially anyone who knew me, and in the case of Principal Butt Hair, hated me.

I slipped into the storage room. It didn't appear to store a whole lot. It was pretty empty except for a few shelves that had a bunch of text books. I figured it was more of a storage facility during the summer when kids weren't using the books. I looked around and immediately spotted an empty roll of duct tape. This was the place.

I dropped my backpack on the floor and removed my materials. I popped open the glue container with my house key. I hadn't brought anything to store the glue in while I rolled so I just dumped a bunch out on the floor and then started spreading it out with the roller. I rolled a thick line across the floor as quickly as I could. I turned back to look at my handy work and realized I had literally painted myself into a corner.

Thankfully, the line was only a few feet thick. With my considerable athletic prowess, I leapt over the glue line and continued pouring and rolling until the entire floor was covered except for the few feet by the front door where I stood.

I packed up my materials and slipped them into my backpack. I pulled the door open a smidge and listened for voices or the squeaking of sneakers. The coast was clear. I speed-walked out of the storage room and hustled to the stairway. I did a quick celebratory dance and headed into my extra help period with Miss Kelvin. I didn't really need it, but it didn't hurt, either. She was a nice teacher and really smart.

Science was pretty uneventful. I basically just sat there hoping for and dreaming about catching the duct tape turds. I had no idea if it would work. They could've had ten different hideouts for all I knew.

Anyway, it was time to head over to middle school. I took the back stairs so that I would pass the supply room. There was a commotion going on outside of the room and I heard angry voices, seemingly from within the room. Excitement surged through my veins.

I didn't want to get too close, for fear of getting caught red-handed (or glue-handed?) with the container of glue or the roller in my backpack. I took off my backpack and held it by my feet as I walked closer to try to keep it out of view from anyone official.

As I got closer to the scene, I heard Principal Buthaire's voice say from inside the room, "Cheeks, just grab my cheeks and pull!"

The crowd grew around the doorway of the supply room, everyone jostling for a better look. I didn't know what to make of it. And then a tearing sound echoed from the room and then the pack jumped back from the doorway as a squeaky scream pierced through the air, "Yowsaaaaaaa!"

The crowd parted quickly as if a duct tape attack was imminent. My heart leapt, but it was Principal Buthaire rushing from the room. He was barefoot and wearing only his boxer shorts (with a strange fish pattern on them), a white undershirt, and half his mustache was gone.

He stormed past me and the rest of the crowd. Laughter echoed throughout the hallway.

I peeked into the room. Two duct tape derelicts stood with panic on their faces halfway into the room. Their sneakers seemingly glued to the floor, they teetered from side to side. Cheeks stood on a piece of cardboard and was attempting to extract the first kid. Principal Buthaire's pants, shirt, and half his mustache were glued to the floor as if he had fallen or been knocked over before the painful extraction that had just taken place.

I almost felt bad about the mustache on account of recently losing both my eyebrows. Almost.

I took one last look into the room, admiring my handywork, and headed off to middle school. I dumped the glue and roller in the dumpster outside the school and rushed to meet Ben and the others in the atrium.

"Anything to report?" Ben asked.

"Mission accomplished. And then some." I leaned in and whispered, "Not only did I glue two perps to the floor, but Butt Hair got stuck, too."

"What?" Sophie yelled.

"Shhh," I said. "And it gets better. They must've knocked him down or he fell because he ran out of the room in his underwear!"

"Oh. My. God." Sophie couldn't believe it. Neither could the rest of them.

"It gets better," I said, laughing.

"How is that possible?" Sammie asked.

"Butt Hair lost half his mustache. It got glued to the floor!"

My whole crew fell into hysterics. It was much needed, following the campaign craziness we had been experiencing.

After we settled down, Cheryl said, "We still have to figure out how to beat Randy."

"He's breaking every rule, using every dirty trick in the book," Sophie added.

"And we still don't have any ideas," I said. "We've had a lot of strategy sessions and a lot of pizza."

"There's nothing wrong with that," Ben said, defensively.

"I agree, but we need to win," I said.

"What about getting the band back together? Randy's promising a performance of his dumb band, Love Puddle." Luke asked.

Sammie said, "But Austin's the lead singer. It's probably going to give him more votes than Sophie."

"But what if we put her up front and let her rip on the guitar? She's crazy good." Luke said.

"I think it's too much of a risk. I think she'll slip in the polls," Cheryl said.

Just Charles said, "We're slip slidin' down. Slippity slip, slidin'."

"That's not very helpful," Cheryl said, shooting eye daggers at Just Charles.

"No. It's very helpful," I said. "Oh, my Gopher! It's gonna be huge."

"What?" Sophie asked, excitedly.

"They won't be able to brand Sophie as the anti-fun candidate once we turn the closed east wing into a giant slip and slide."

"What?" Ben asked. "Dude, that's crazy. Even for you."

"Is it though?" I asked.

"It is," Sophie said. "But it's just crazy enough to work."

"I'll help organize, but I won't be in attendance," I said.

"Game on, Warblemacher," Sophie said with a smile. It was good to see her excited about the election. It had been a serious downer, almost from minute one.

25

I t was time for Sophie to slip and slide to election victory. With the crew's help, we were able to use the plastic that was meant to seal up all the classrooms for a greater purpose. And more fun. We lined the east wing hallway with plastic and even created a makeshift tube out of it that we ran from Max's deserted bathroom's faucet. Everyone would be sliding in the direction of the exit doors at the end of the hallway with any excess water flowing that way.

We used trusted associates to spread the word with limited detail about who or what was going on. All anyone knew was that if you wanted to be involved in the coolest event of the year, you had to be in the east wing immediately after eighth period. And it was invite only. They were to tell no one. So, of course, everybody knew.

From what I am told, nearly a hundred kids from the eighth grade showed up just after the bell. They all crowded just inside the plastic wall as Sophie addressed them. She said, "Who says you can't have great ideas and have fun at the same time!" and then proceeded to run and dive onto the slip and slide, fully clothed in jeans and a sweatshirt.

Ben, Just Charles, Luke, and even Cheryl, who can sometimes be a little uptight, followed her, which was just enough social proof to suggest to the rest of the kids there that it was a great idea. Before they knew it, four or five kids at a time rushed down the slip and slide.

Water splashed everywhere. Kids were crashing into each other and the walls, screaming and having a blast. It ended quickly, though, which was fine, because the buses were about to leave, anyway. Zorch and a security guard slipped into the closed-off area.

Zorch said angrily, "Hey! What's going on?"

Kids scattered. If you thought it was chaos when the kids were slip sliding for fun, imagine how crazy it was when they were all trying to avoid capture. But they did. Every single one of them slip-slided out of the exit doors to freedom and either onto the buses or off to Frank's if they didn't make it to the bus. Still, eating pizza while sopping wet isn't the worst thing that could happen to you.

I was waiting for the crew at Frank's, a steaming pizza ready to go for their arrival. Sophie and Cheryl came in first, soaking wet and loving every minute of it. They rushed over to me, giddy, with Ben, Just Charles, and Luke close behind.

Sophie jumped into my arms, nearly knocking me down.

"That was so amazing! What a great idea!" Sophie yelled.

"What happened?" I asked, excited.

They told me the story and then dried off with the hand dryers in the bathroom before helping me finish the pizza that I couldn't wait to start.

THE EVEN MORE FABULOUS news was the next day's polling data that hit, fueled a solid jump for Sophie.

We sat at lunch while Cheryl read the most recent poll to us. "The staff at the Gazette just compiled this. Sophie's climbing, while Austin slipped a little. Sophie cut into Randy by 8% and Austin by 5%. It's now 35%, 29%, and 28%."

Ben looked at me and said, "Don't worry about it, dude. I'm sure you'll make it back."

"I'm trying to lose!"

"Oh, yeah. You'll totally continue to mess this up. I have faith in you."

"I'm confused," I said.

"Me, too," Ben said.

"We all are," Sophie said.

"The slip and slide seemed to overshadow the poster defamation that the Pretty Posse has been hard at work on," Cheryl said.

"What poster defamation?" I asked. "I haven't seen anything."

One of Sophie's posters by the library had a unibrow added to it and two teeth were blackened out."

"That's not right," Sophie said, annoyed.

Cheryl continued, "Not sure why anyone bothered to mess with Lyla's campaign, given that she's only pulling 2% of the vote, but somebody thought it was funny to draw a giant snot bubble coming out of her nose on one of her posters."

"That sounds kinda funny," Luke said.

"It's not," Sophie said.

"It's snot?" I asked.

Sophie looked at Cheryl and shook her head. "Honestly, does it get any better than this?"

"My mom told me, no. My dad still tells fart jokes."

"Ugh."

"What do we do about the Posse and Randy?" I asked. Even though Sophie's campaign was on the upswing, we still needed to figure out a way to take Randy down a few notches.

"I still think we need to shift some votes from Austin to Sophie," Cheryl said, tapping her chin. "Nobody who would vote for Austin would vote for Randy."

"Some might go the dude route and vote for Zack," Ben added.

"Even if half of my votes went to Zack and you split with Lyla, which you should get more, you would beat Randy."

"But we've tried to get people not to vote for you. The

harder we try to deter them, the more they want to vote for you," Sophie said to me.

"We can still try to knock Randy down. There's got to be something," Ben said.

"What has he promised that we can prove he's lying? What about the party?" I asked.

"We don't know anything about it," Sophie said. "He was very vague on details."

"Which has me thinking he was lying about it. Maybe Derek knows something," I said.

26

After dinner, Derek was watching videos on YouTube while sitting on the couch in the den. I walked and stood in front of him. Derek didn't budge as he chuckled. A poor skate boarder probably just fell down a flight of stairs or something.

"Hey," I said. Derek looked up at me. "Did you hear any details about Randy's party?"

"Sorry, dude. You're not on the list."

"How do you know?" I asked.

"Really?"

"Ok, fine. You're right."

"I know," Derek said, getting up and walking away.

"Just tell me where it is," I said, annoyed.

"Nope."

I shook my head as he left the room. And then I had an idea. I walked over to my mom's home office and peeked my head in.

"Hey, ma?" I said.

"Yeah, honey," she said, looking up at me from her desk.

"One of the kids at school was talking about how cool

the new BBQ place is on Main Street. Is that the place Derek is going for Randy's party?"

She thought for a minute, "No, I think he said it was at The Zone."

"Oh, okay. Thanks."

"Do you want to go to the BBQ place and give it a try?"

"Sure," I said. I'll never pass up good BBQ. "Thanks. Do you think you can take me to The Zone? I want to check out some stuff for Sophie's campaign.

"Dad's going to pick up Leighton in a bit. He can probably take you on the way."

"Thanks!"

MY DAD DROVE me over to The Zone. It wasn't too crowded, being that it was after dinner in the middle of the week. My dad held the door for me and then we walked inside together.

"Do you need my help?" my dad asked.

"Nah, I got this. You can chill over there," I said, nodding to a waiting area off to the side. "Thanks."

"No problem," he said, heading over to a cozy-looking chair.

I walked up to the young woman behind the podium.

"Hi there! Can I help you?" she asked, sweetly.

"Hi," I said, nervously. "I'm running a school election campaign for a friend of mine." I nearly threw up in my mouth referring to Randy as my friend. "He's hosting a party after the election. My dad just took me over here to pick up the contract."

The woman furrowed her brow. "That doesn't sound

familiar. What's the name?" she asked, while opening a book.

I leaned in and said softly, "Warblemacher."

"That definitely doesn't sound familiar." She scanned the page with her finger.

"Could it be under another name?"

I shrugged. "Maybe Storm?"

She looked again. "No. I'm sorry. There must've been a communication mix-up with your friend."

"Hmm," I said, stalling. I had an idea. I took out my phone and said, "Let me check my notes." I held my phone up so she couldn't see and clicked my video camera on. I pretended to scroll. "So, you're saying that Randy Warblemacher did not book a party here at The Zone, even though he promised everyone at school that he did?"

"I don't know what he promised, but there is no party planned for Warblemacher or Stone. We're booked solid for the next three months. And we have been since the summer."

I smiled and shut off my phone. "Thank you very much."

"I'm sorry I couldn't be more helpful," she said.

"You've been so helpful, you have no idea." I smiled again and headed over to my dad.

"Got everything you need?" he asked.

"And then some," I said.

27

The video went out the next morning to all the social media channels. Kids were not happy. It spread like wildfire. We couldn't wait to hear about the updated polling data. We thought it could be the knockout blow we were looking for.

Cheryl was the last to arrive at lunch. She slid her tray onto the table with excitement in her eyes. It wasn't the typical entrance we'd experienced during the campaign, or really anyone entering the cafeteria during lunch ever.

"Polling data is improving. We picked up another two points!" Cheryl said.

"Great news," Sophie said, like it wasn't great news.

"What's wrong?" Cheryl asked.

"Two points isn't going to win," Sophie said.

"Even with the video?" I asked, confused.

"Well, Randy's down by 5%, but Sophie only picked up 2% of it."

"What?" I couldn't believe it.

"Can we talk about something different just for today?" Sophie asked.

"Sure," Cheryl said.

Nobody apparently knew what to say besides talk about the election, so we sat there for a few minutes in silence.

I broke the ice. "Why did you get the tuna pot pie?" I asked. "It just sounds terrible. Even the stuff that sounds good tastes terrible."

Sophie shrugged. "At least it's hot. It's gotta kill most of the bacteria, right?"

"I guess," I said.

"So, I lodged a complaint with Ms. Pierre about the food quality. I haven't heard back. I'm sure she'll ignore it. She pretends to be nicer than Principal Buthaire, but she's really not."

As she continued to bash Ms. Pierre, I looked up to see Ms. Pierre walking through the cafeteria and she was within earshot. In a panic, I elbowed Sophie to get her to stop talking.

For a second, I thought it worked. And I guess it did, because she stopped talking, but there was a bigger problem. She also stopped breathing.

Sophie stood up, her face registering panic, as she put both hands to her neck, signaling that she was choking. I hopped up out of my seat without a second thought and wrapped my arms around her from behind. My first aid training from the Cub Scouts kicked into high gear. I pulled my hands toward me, giving Sophie the Heimlich maneuver. It didn't work. I tried it again as everyone around me panicked.

Cheryl yelled, "Do something!"

"I am!"

I pulled harder. I heard a pop and then a huge gasp of air, and then watched as a huge piece of tuna soared through the air, en route to Ms. Pierre. Her head turned in our direction, her ninja senses apparently alerting her to the deadly tuna hurdling in her direction at near warp speed.

Ms. Pierre turned her hips and rotated her body toward the incoming tuna. With a primal scream and a deadly ridge hand attack, she pulverized the tuna.

Not one piece of tuna or pot pie remained. My science genius brain tried to make sense of what I had just seen. The force of the attack literally vaporized the tuna. I couldn't believe it, and then remembered Sophie had been choking.

"Are you okay?" I asked.

Sophie was more embarrassed than anything at that point. She was breathing fine. Her ego was probably a little bruised, but she was physically fine.

Ms. Pierre straightened her jacket and walked toward us.

"Holy farts, she's coming this way," I whispered.

Sophie's face turned white.

"Say something," she said.

"You say something. I didn't just spit my lunch at her," I said. I know, I'm a real romantic.

Ms. Pierre stopped in front of our table and stared at us. As did the rest of the cafeteria.

"Ms. Pierre, I'm really sorry about that. I was choking. Austin gave me the Heimlich."

"It's okay. Just don't let it happen again, Miss Rodriguez."

"I won't," Sophie said.

WITHIN AN HOUR, a meme on social media was going around to all the kids. It had a photoshopped picture of me on a fireman's body, saving a baby from a burning building.

It wasn't good. Cheryl walked up to Sophie, Ben, and me at the end of the day before we headed out to the buses. She looked like her grandmother died or something.

"Is everything okay?" Ben asked. "You look depressed."

"No. Everything is not okay, Benjamin. We're just getting creamed."

"Just tell me the numbers and get it over with," Sophie said.

"We have a new candidate in the lead. Austin has 38% of the vote. Randy's at 36% and Sophie's at 24%."

"How did Randy gain votes when Austin saved me?" Sophie said.

"Choking shows weakness," Cheryl said.

"What? Are you serious?" Sophie yelled.

"Unfortunately, the in-depth questionnaire I circulated confirmed it."

"Do you know how many people that tuna pot pie nearly killed yesterday?" I asked.

"I think six," Cheryl said.

"Really? That's only an average near-death day. I would've thought it was more," I said.

Sophie looked drained. Her eyes were watery once again. "Maybe we should just have you try to beat him," she whispered. "I'd rather you be president than Randy. I'm not cut out for this."

"What are you talking about?" I asked.

"I never knew I cared so much about what other people thought about me. I'm weak. I'm choking on popularity. Or lack of it."

"Let's not use the word, 'choke.'" Cheryl said.

"Nope," I said. "You're gonna be our president. But maybe I *should* try. Then I'll lose votes. Or at least that seems to be how it works. Maybe I should just drop out of school," I said, chuckling.

"I never would've guessed that you saving my life would be such a downer," Sophie said. She shook her head, "He's trying to lose and he's still better than me. Why does everybody hate me?" Sophie was spiraling.

"Nobody hates you," I said softly, while rubbing her shoulder.

"Well, they don't like what I have to offer," she said.

"Did you ever ask them?" Ben asked.

"What to offer? No. I just made my platform about what I thought people wanted. About what I wanted." Sophie's face brightened as her shoulders straightened up. "I know what I'm gonna do."

28

Sophie was over at my house after dinner. Derek and Leighton were out, so it was quiet. We sat in my den trying to figure out what she should say in her final speech. I couldn't believe Election Day was coming up. We needed to have a big week.

"What do you offer that Randy can't?" I asked.

"Everything good," Sophie answered.

"True, but what?"

"I don't know. Kindness?"

"That's great," I said.

My dad interrupted. "Everything good in here?"

I think so. Just trying to figure out how to make Sophie's campaign stand out. We don't know what she should say to win."

"You can't control who wins," he said.

"Why not?" I asked.

My dad chuckled. "Because you can't force someone to write your name down on the ballot. It's in the voter's hands. You can only focus on you and what you're going to do. Just be you."

"They don't seem to like me," Sophie said.

"That's not true, but even if it were, we all know you're amazing. If they don't see it, they just have bad eyesight. Popularity is out of your control. Everybody wants to be liked, but you can't make someone like you."

"But people don't like Regan," I said.

"Yeah, they suck up to her because they're afraid of her wrath."

"That's not friendship. That's not popularity. You have to do what's right," my dad said.

"But Randy's telling so many lies," I added.

"You just have to hope that the kids see through the lies."

"I'm not that hopeful," I said.

"Don't stoop to his level."

"Then we lose," Sophie said.

"Do you? If you do what's right, you can't lose."

Sophie and I both thought about that for a minute.

My dad asked, "Did you say something about kindness before?"

"Yeah. Randy and his friends are all about tearing people down. We need more kindness."

"That's great. Figure out a way to do something with that." My dad looked at me. "I don't think I've ever told you this story. It's important for you both to understand. And all kids, really. You're at the age where you seem to care the most about what other people think about you. The best day of my life outside of when your mother and I got married and you, your sister, and your brother were born-"

"Having Derek was one of the best days of your life? Have you changed that opinion yet?"

"Very funny," my dad said, chuckling. "But this is important. One of the top five days of my life was the day I stopped caring what other people thought about me."

"You don't care what other people think?" I asked.

"If I know I'm right- if I know I'm living my life right, why does it matter what anyone else thinks? Why would you let someone else affect your opinion of you? Kids seem to care more about what their friends and enemies think than what they think about themselves."

"Or let other kids affect how we think about ourselves," Sophie said. "That's been happening to me since the election started."

"It happens to me all the time. You think it's easy being picked on by Randy or Butt Hair all the time?"

"You get picked on by Butt Hair? That's just weird," my dad said, laughing.

"Funny," I said.

"It happens to everyone. Austin, you're one of the strongest kids I know. I don't care that you're not on the football team. Even Nick DeRozan isn't as strong as you. You stand up for yourself and your friends like no kid I've ever known. And Sophie, what I know about you is that you're just as strong."

I nodded, soaking it all in.

My dad finished by saying, "We're proud of you, win or lose, because you're giving it your best and doing it the right way. It doesn't matter how many votes you get in the end. Just give it your best."

29

The next morning, Randy picked the wrong girl to mess with. He walked by, heading to his idiot crew. Randy did a double take when he saw Sophie and me.

"Mr. and Mrs. Davenfart, a displeasure, as always. Tired of losing yet?"

"No, just tired of your false promises, lies, and attacks," Sophie said.

Randy flashed his best smile, as he stepped closer to us. "Here's what I'll do because I'm a good guy and all. Drop out of the race and I'll make sure the negativity stops."

"Pass. Three days before the election? You want me to tell everyone I'm out? No thank you. But thanks for being a good guy and all," she said, sarcastically. "You sic your attack dogs on me and expect me to think you're a good guy when you call them off? You're an idiot and I'm going to crush you." Sophie said, storming off, determined.

"You're gonna regret this," Randy called after her. "You can't beat me! I'm unbeatable!"

"You got burned, Randolph," I said, following Sophie.

Sophie walked over to Cheryl, who was setting up a table with a few chairs on the side of the Atrium.

"You have the sign?" Sophie turned and asked me, all business.

"Yep," I said, handing it to her. "And the duct tape?"

"That's a sore subject," I said.

"Even after the big victory?" Ben asked.

"Yes, the nightmares won't ever go away," I said, holding in a smile.

Ben grabbed the sign from Sophie as Just Charles tore off a piece of tape. He hung it in front of the table. It read, 'Power to the People- What do you want?'

Jamie Gribben looked over at us and then around the atrium. She walked over to us slowly, seemingly unsure of what we were doing and if she should be seen talking to us.

"Hey, Jamie!" Sophie said, enthusiastically.

I thought it might scare her off, but Jamie smiled and fully committed to stepping up to the table.

"What are you doing?" Jamie asked.

"I want to build my campaign around what the students want. Of course, we all want less homework and no tests, but Randy's promises aren't realistic. What's something that you want that is really possible for me to achieve?"

"I don't know," Jamie said, playing with her long, brown hair. "An extra minute in between classes. It's really hard to get from the west wing to the new portable classrooms now that the east wing is closed."

"That makes sense," Sophie said. "Anything else?"

"Umm, less time on the bus," Jamie said.

"Okay," Sophie said, as Cheryl typed everything into her laptop.

"Thanks for sharing," Sophie said.

"Good luck," Jamie said. "I really hope you win." She looked at me and said, "No offense."

"None taken. I'm trying to lose."

It was awesome. After Jamie walked away, it was like the floodgates opened up. Sophie's campaign had a buzz for the first time since she signed up. Kids were coming up left and right, sharing ideas and telling Sophie what a great job she'll do. Sophie needed it.

I smiled at Randy and Regan, who watched from across the Atrium. Regan said something to Amy Guarino, who then walked away, annoyed. I watched curiously as Amy walked toward us. She joined a circle of kids that surrounded Sophie, who talked animatedly.

Sophie smiled at Amy and asked, "What do you think?"

Amy took a sip of her fruit punch and said, "Here's what I think." She proceeded to dump the bottle of fruit punch on top of Sophie's head. The fruit punch filled her hair and ran down her face and neck, soaking and staining her white shirt with a sea of red.

Sophie's shock wore off quickly. Most of us were still in shock, too, but some kids laughed, while others pointed, not believing what they had just seen. Sophie started sobbing and ran off. Cheryl was right behind her.

I looked over to see Randy and Regan, cracking up with the Pretty Posse. I had about enough. Nobody had the right to do that to anyone. And the fact that it was my girlfriend and they had been relentless in torturing her, just made me that much angrier.

I stormed over to Randy. Ben, Just Charles, and Luke were right behind me.

"Dude," Ben yelled. "What are you gonna do?"

I didn't answer him. I was too angry. And I didn't really know. I just knew that I had to do something. I walked up to Randy and stopped in front of him.

"Can I help you, Davenfart?" Randy said, with a fake smile.

"You've gone too far, Randy," I said, shaking.

"What are you gonna do about it?" Randy chuckled.

"The little baby looks like he's gonna have a tantrum," Regan said. "Or maybe he just has to make a poopie."

Randy and the Pretty Posse laughed.

"I'm so tired of you. You're such a jerk, I don't even know why your mother likes you. We're going to beat you so bad in the election, you're going to be embarrassed for the rest of your life."

"How are you gonna do that?" Randy asked.

"Haven't figured that part out just yet, but rest assured, it's comin' atcha. We're gonna get ya. I'm willing to do whatever it takes."

Randy reached forward and nudged my shoulder. "Get outta here, Davenfart, before you get yourself hurt."

"You don't want to mess with me today. I'll bite if I have to."

Just Charles added, "Yeah, me too."

It was kinda weird, but it broke some of tension.

"Enough is enough, Randy," I said, walking away.

Randy and Regan laughed as we headed back to the table. People stared at me. Some even congratulated me, but I was too angry to respond. I just kept my gaze focused on the table. Sophie wasn't back yet. I wasn't sure if she would come back.

"I'll meet you back here," I said to Ben and Just Charles. "Keep listening to ideas. We're not stopping because they want us to stop."

I found Sophie, Sammie, and Cheryl. They were sitting against the wall outside the girls' bathroom.

"Can I join?" I asked, softly.

Sophie nodded. I slid down the wall and sat next to Cheryl. Sophie and Sammie were to her left.

"We need to change the direction of this campaign," Cheryl said.

"Into the toilet isn't working?" Sophie asked. She laughed, but it was more sarcastic than joyful. Like a lot more. "The campaign is over. I'm done."

I leaned over and looked at Sophie. "There are only a few days left. You were making progress."

"Yeah, you just need to stand up to the Pretty Posse," Sammie said.

"Chick Clique is just so much better. I really think they missed a great branding opportunity."

"Well, that's a good thing, right?" Cheryl asked.

"I guess so," I said. "Soph, Sammie's right. You need to stand up to them. You need to get back out there and show them that you're not afraid of them. Because everyone else is."

"But I have fruit punch all over my white shirt. My hair is a mess. I look like an idiot," Sophie said.

"And still, you're beautiful," I said. "But it doesn't matter. Roll your sleeves up and get back to work, Madam President!"

Mr. Muscalini walked by and said, "That's right! Roll those sleeves up! Sun's out, guns out, people!"

I like to think that it was what I said and not Mr. Muscalini's shallow, seasonal slogan that got Sophie up off the floor, heading back to the Atrium. She wiped her eyes and looked over at me. I'd seen that look before. And I liked it. It was the same look she had when she took out Randy and Regan at the Medieval Renaissance Fair.

Sophie power-walked her way to the Atrium. She walked so fast; I couldn't keep up. When we got back, a Pretty Posse had formed near the table, which meant the voting public was sparse. I looked around and everybody seemed to be afraid of the Posse. Sophie headed straight for them.

"What is she doing?" I said to Cheryl. "She's on a collision course! This isn't gonna end well."

"You told her to stand up to them," Cheryl said, confused.

"Oh, yeah. But, still. She could just yell at them from across the room."

30

Sophie walked right through the Posse, pushing Jasmine Jane and Ditzy Dayna to the side, and walked right into the eye of the storm. She was nose to nose with Regan. I don't know what she said, but Sophie pushed Regan to the side and walked past, head high, and back to the table. Everyone just stared at her.

Sammie, Cheryl, and I met Sophie and the others back at the table.

Sophie took a deep breath, and stared down Regan. She refocused and said, "Maybe we should start a kindness club. I think we could use one right about now. What do you guys think?"

"I think it's a great idea. Why not ask them?" Cheryl asked.

"How?" Sophie asked. She looked around at the crowd. Then without waiting for a response, she climbed up onto the table. Her normally curly hair was matted down. She had psychedelic fruit punch patterns on her shirt, but it didn't matter. Her voice boomed, "Hi everyone. I'm Sophie

Rodriguez. I want to tell you how disgusted I am by how we're treating each other during this election."

All Atrium eyes were on Sophie, as she continued, "I'm running for president, but I don't care if I win or not. I'm starting a kindness club where kids can go to support each other and help others, not to tear them down. I don't need to win an election to do that." Sophie made a point to stare extra-long at Regan and her Pretty Posse. A bunch of kids started to cheer.

"You can sign up here if you'd like to join," Sophie said, pointing to the table.

Ditzy Dayna walked away from the Posse. She glanced back at Regan and then headed over to the table.

Regan yelled, "Don't think you're ever coming back!"

Dayna grabbed a pen from Sammie and signed the sheet of paper. She turned to Sophie and then looked down at the ground.

"I'm sorry," she whispered.

Sophie walked toward Dayna and gave her a hug.

"It's okay," Sophie said.

A bunch of kids walked over, waiting to sign up.

Regan stormed off, the Pretty Posse following close behind.

"That was awesome," Cheryl said. "It's gonna poll huge!"

"I don't care," Sophie said. "I didn't do that to win. I did it because it was the right thing to do and needed to be done."

WE WERE in the home stretch. It was Tuesday, just before the final speeches. It was the final formal part of the campaign. Then there would be two more days of hitting the campaign trail with Election Day on Friday.

Cheryl had stopped telling Sophie what the polling numbers were, but she kept me up to date. After Sophie started the kindness club, her numbers started to climb, but most of the votes she took were from me. So, she hadn't passed Randy.

I chose not to give a speech. Neither did Lyla or Zack. I hoped I was making the right decision. I seemed to win votes no matter what I did. I fell on my face and knocked over the podium. I skipped the debates. I told them flat out that I didn't want their votes. I even sent around videos of my armpit hair. I had lost faith in the ability of the voting public to make the right decision. But there was nothing I could do. Only Sophie could make them vote for Sophie.

And it was time for her to attempt to do that. I sat in the audience with our crew near the front of the auditorium. Sophie stood in front of the podium as she looked out at the quiet audience. I didn't know what she was going to say. She worked on the speech by herself.

Sophie took a deep breath and then said, "I've learned a lot throughout this election. I've learned that I have great friends who will always support me and believe in me, even when I don't believe in myself."

My crew clapped like crazy. Sammie yelled, "We got you, girl!"

Sophie smiled, and continued, "I also learned that there are people who are not as supportive as my friends. And they will lie and make things up about me or you to make themselves feel better about themselves. We may expect girls to gossip, form chick cliques," Sophie said, smiling at me, "and tear each other down, but we don't have to accept it. Others' treatment of you is a reflection of them, not you."

A lot of people started clapping. I looked over to the side

of the stage to see Randy smirking like an idiot. He just didn't get it.

"And I will not allow anyone to determine my self worth, but me. And you shouldn't, either. I've learned that it doesn't matter what anyone thinks about you. It only matters what you think about yourself. I thought I needed hundreds of votes to win this election. It turns out that I only need one vote to win. My own. And you only need your own."

The crowd, both teachers and students, cheered like crazy. I jumped to my feet and yelled, "Sophie for President!"

Nearly everyone in the entire audience rose to their feet, clapping like crazy. A chant broke out. "So-Phie! So-Phie! So-Phie!"

After the cheering died down, Randy and Sophie

switched places. Randy adjusted the microphone and cleared his throat.

"My name is Randy Warblemacher and I'm your president of the eighth-grade class. And I'm here to tell you why. I know what you want and I'm going to fight for those things. As your president, I will change the grading scale. Nobody will get less than a 'C.'"

The crowd cheered. I leaned over to Ben and said, "Here we go again. He's going to promise stuff he has no way of giving them, but they won't care."

Randy continued, "Attendance will be optional. Students should get paid if we show up. Teachers get paid to show up. Why shouldn't we?"

The crowd cheered again. I looked around at them and just shook my head.

"And while we're on the subject of teachers, I think they should get report cards from us! And why shouldn't we be able to call them by their first names? These are just some of the things that I will do for you as your president!" Randy looked out at the crowd. People were cheering, but not going crazy like they did for Sophie. He thrust his fist in the air and yelled, "I have a dream!"

The crowd jumped to its feet and cheered like crazy.

Ben said to me, "I thought school was to teach these boneheads not to be such idiots?"

I just shook my head, shocked at the stupidity of my fellow classmates.

After the auditorium let out, I fought my way to Sophie, who was surrounded by people congratulating her. When she saw me, she excused herself and headed toward me.

She jumped into my arms, nearly knocking me over.

"That. Was. So. Amazing," I said.

Somebody walked by and said, "Good luck. I know you're gonna win."

"Thanks," Sophie said, and then to me, "I already did."

"Yep. It just takes one vote."

31

I t was Election Day. The graduating Cherry Avenue Middle School Gophers would exercise their rights to choose a leader (I use this term loosely should Randy win) for the remainder of eighth grade. I nerd-ran from high school to the middle school that morning. I wanted as much time in the Atrium as possible, so that I could campaign. Every vote mattered and I was determined to help Sophie win.

Our crew stood together, waiting for Cheryl to arrive with the latest polling data. We would use it to determine who to focus our time on.

Cheryl ran over to us, out of breath.

Ben asked, "How do the polls look?"

Sammie asked, "How close is it?"

"I don't know," Cheryl said, shrugging. "The only thing we know is that kids are sick of being polled."

"That's unfortunate," Sophie said. "What now, Chief Strategist?"

I thought for a moment. "They're focusing on individuals. Let's focus on a higher level. Groups. We can totally win back the photography club," I said. "You just gotta play up that Randy lied about the new equipment."

"I can handle that," Just Charles said. "Steve Alonso is the V.P. He's in my math class."

"And the chess club?" Cheryl asked.

"In the bag already," Ben said. "Not voting for Randy."

"But are they voting for Sophie?" I asked.

"I'll make sure. They do idolize you," Ben said to me.

"Nobody said they had bad taste. We just want them to point it in the right direction."

"Just to be clear- nobody in the chess club will be trying to taste me? Remember when Brad Melon wanted to lick you?" Sophie asked.

"No. And no," I said, firmly.

"Any sports teams that we can turn?" Luke asked.

"Boys volleyball and lacrosse are possible," Just Charles said.

"Yeah, work on any sport that's not football, basketball, or baseball. He probably parades around the locker room, gym, and fields like he's better than the rest of them."

The advisory bell rang.

"Sounds like a plan," Cheryl said.

"Thanks, guys. You're the best," Sophie said.

EVERYONE WHO WANTED to vote could do so during lunch. As soon as it was my turn, I rushed to the gym. What I saw didn't make me happy. Nick DeRozan stood outside the gym doors. When he saw me, he stepped to the side and let me pass, but I didn't feel good about it, so before I went to vote, I stayed close, to see what he was doing.

It wasn't good. Gary Larkin walked up to the gym doors.

Nick DeRozan stepped in front of him, blocking the way.

Nick folded his arms and said, "You're late for lunch."

Gary stared up at Nick's hulking body and said, "Umm, you're, you're right."

I rushed over to Dr. Dinkledorf. "Sir! We have a huge problem. Nick DeRozan is suppressing voters! He just told Gary Larkin to go back to lunch before he voted. This isn't right!"

Dr. Dinkledorf walked quickly, well, as quickly as he was capable of walking, and disappeared through the door.

"Mr. DeRozan, where are you supposed to be?"

"I have gym now, but it's closed for voting."

"So, you're intimidating voters?"

"I, umm, no."

"Well, let's head down to Ms. Pierre's office for a little chit chat."

I shook my head as they walked away. I didn't know what to do about it. So, I voted. How many kids were turned away? The polling was pretty close to begin with. Sophie couldn't give votes away to Randy.

I didn't know what to tell Sophie. And then I saw her approaching with a smile on her face.

"How's it going?" she asked.

"Great!" I lied. "I just voted. You seem happy."

"I can't control what happens. I already cast the winning vote, remember? And if I don't win, I can still accomplish what I want. We can fight for better food in the cafeteria. We can start the kindness club. We can slash all the tires on the buses, so kids have to walk to school to get more exercise."

Mr. Muscalini was walking by and yelled, "I'll help with that!"

"I was kidding, sir," Sophie said.

"Well, I might do it anyway!"

I WAS on edge the next few periods. Outside of the issue with Nick, I hadn't heard of anything crazy happening. Apparently, a few seventh-grade football players tried to vote a year early, but were turned away. I wondered what else Randy could've done to turn the tides without us knowing. I was driving myself crazy until I remembered what Sophie said about not being able to control any of it. I just couldn't wait to find out already.

As I sat in English, the Speaker of Doom crackled. "At the end of the period, all eighth graders, please report to the auditorium for the election announcement."

After the bell rang, I headed to the auditorium. All of the candidates stood backstage while the crowd assembled in the auditorium. Voices and laughter echoed throughout the room. None of it came from the five candidates. Even Randy and his oversized and under deserved ego were quiet.

I watched the other candidates as we all awaited our election fates. Randy paced in a circle, staring at his feet with his hands behind his back. Sophie stood with her eyes closed, breathing deeply. Zack ran his fingers up and down his non-existent mustache while Lyla blew her nose so hard into a tissue, I thought she may have shot out some brain, too. I guess she didn't want any snot bubble trouble.

Dr. Dinkledorf slid by our group without saying a word. He was not wearing his Lincoln hat or beard. I didn't know if that was a good sign or not. The election certainly wasn't as fun as we all thought it would be. Maybe for Randy, it was, but I didn't really care if he enjoyed it or not.

Dr. Dinkledorf walked up to the podium and tapped the microphone. "Good afternoon, everyone. We're here to announce your class president as elected by you, the students.

It was a hard-fought battle. There were ups and downs, and it was our most competitive race in nearly twenty years, but the candidates should be proud of themselves, and you should be thankful that these leaders chose to step up to serve."

"Get on with it, old man!" someone yelled from the crowd. I'm sure it was one of Randy's supporters.

Dr. Dinkledorf said, "So, without any further ado, your eighth-grade class president..."

The auditorium was the most silent I had ever heard it. Well, you know what I mean.

Dr.   Dinkledorf   continued,   "...is   President Rrrrrodriguez!"

The crowd erupted into cheers, as Sophie nearly fell over. But she got a second wind after a moment. She jumped into my arms.

"You gotta get out there! The people want to meet their president!" I said.

"Thank you!" Sophie said, tears welling up in her eyes. Finally, they were good tears.

Dr. Dinkledorf walked over to us, as Sophie readied herself to deliver a victory speech that she hadn't written just yet.

Randy walked away, kicked a chair, groaned, and then kicked another chair. That was, of course, followed by another groan.

"I'm sorry things didn't work out better for you all," Dr. Dinkledorf said, patting me on the shoulder. "You should be proud that you gave your best. Only five of you had the guts to stand up and do this. There's something to be said for that. Where's Randy?"

"On his way to the foot doctor," I said.

Dr. Dinkledorf frowned. "Well, does anyone want to make a concession speech? You can congratulate Sophie and thank your supporters?"

Lyla wiped a tear from her eye. "I don't think so. I haven't blown my nose recently and I ran out of tissues."

"I'm good," I said. "I think we reached the school spending limit on podiums already this year."

Dr. Dinkledorf laughed. "And you, Zack?"

"Yeah, I'd like to say something."

Zack stepped up to the microphone. He looked like he was actually thinking about what to say. I readied myself for something intelligent. Zack simply said, "It was your mustake!" And then gave himself a finger mustache.

"Great speech," Sophie said, as she walked past Zack on her way to the podium.

"You got lucky, Sophie," he said.

I nearly fell over laughing. The crowd started cheering as Sophie stepped up to the microphone.

"Thank you, everyone. I didn't prepare a speech, so I just want to say, thank you to everyone who voted for me. I promise to give you my best. Thank you to my friends who helped me throughout this campaign. And to my boyfriend, Austin-"

Regan stood up and yelled, "Boo! We want a recount!" She looked around, expecting support. Nobody cheered. Nobody booed along with her. They all just stared at her. Or stared away from her.

Regan looked at Jasmine. "Hey! What's wrong with you?"

Jasmine stood up and said, "What's wrong with you?" She scooted out of the row and headed toward the exit. Other members of the Posse followed Jasmine to the doors.

Regan looked around exasperated. "You're gonna regret this!"

Sophie chimed in, "No, they won't. Because they see through you. This invitation is to you, Regan, and the rest of you as well. If you would like to choose kindness over catty cliques-" Sophie stopped her speech and looked over at me. "Ooh, that's a good one, right?"

I gave her a thumbs up.

Sophie continued, "I mean, you can join us in the kindness club. We'll be meeting at Frank's Pizza every Tuesday after school until it becomes a sanctioned club here. Cherry Avenue Middle School Gophers rule!"

The crowd jumped to their feet and cheered. Regan stormed out of the back of the auditorium.

IT WAS the first day of a new era. Sophie Rodriguez was our

eighth-grade class president and I couldn't be happier. I walked into the atrium after science class at the high school. I was late for advisory class, so the atrium was empty. I was a little disappointed I wasn't able to see the buzz around Sophie and hear the congratulations, but I had the whole year to enjoy it.

The campaign posters were still up on the wall. I looked over and shook my head, remembering all the craziness. And then I stopped dead in my tracks. There was a new poster up on the wall. It was a picture of me. There was long hair drawn on it with lipstick and earrings. Underneath the picture, it read, 'Congrats to our new (First- crossed out) Fart Lady, Austin Davenfart!'

"Ahhh, farts," I said. Randy had struck again. The guy never quit, but we had survived his election misdirection, and lived to fart, er fight, another day.

Got Audio?

Want to listen to Middle School Mayhem?

ABOUT THE AUTHOR

C.T. Walsh is the author of the Middle School Mayhem Series, set to be a total twelve hilarious adventures of Austin Davenport and his friends.

Besides writing fun, snarky humor and the occasionally-frequent fart joke, C.T. loves spending time with his family, coaching his kids' various sports, and successfully turning seemingly unsandwichable things into spectacular sandwiches, while also claiming that he never eats carbs. He assures you, it's not easy to do. C.T. knows what you're thinking: this guy sounds complex, a little bit mysterious, and maybe even dashingly handsome, if you haven't been to the optometrist in a while. And you might be right.

C.T. finds it weird to write about himself in the third person, so he is going to stop doing that now.

You can learn more about C.T. (oops) at ctwalsh.fun

 facebook.com/ctwalshauthor

ALSO BY C.T. WALSH

Down with the Dance: Book One

Santukkah!: Book Two

The Science (Un)Fair: Book Three

Battle of the Bands: Book Four

Medieval Mayhem: Book Five

The Takedown: Book Six

Valentine's Duh: Book Seven

The Comic Con: Book Eight

Future Release schedule

Education: Domestication: August 15th, 2020

Class Tripped: September 15th, 2020

Graduation Detonation: November 15th, 2020